"Connolly's narrative is full of meaningful moral lessons—on the limits of loyalty, the importance of honesty, and the absolute necessity of trusting others…an enchanting new juvenile fantasy series."

—*Foreword Reviews* on *Shadow Weaver*

"This book contains plenty of action and intrigue to keep the reader turning pages. It is quick to read and contains enough unsolved mysteries to make the reader look forward to the next title in the series."

—*School Library Connection* on *Shadow Weaver*

"The theme of friendship is handled deftly here… A gripping finale reveals the truth about the 'cure' for magic, and readers will eagerly anticipate learning more."

—*Bulletin of the Center for Children's Books* on *Shadow Weaver*

★ "Connolly again spins a magical tale; she deftly crafts moods and creates a sense of urgency that will leave readers breathless. The conclusion to the duology brings a feeling of relief, but a few puzzling questions remain, leaving the door ajar for future adventures."

—*Booklist*, Starred Review on *Comet Rising*

# HOLLOW DOLLS

# HOLLOW DOLLS

## MarcyKate Connolly

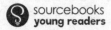
sourcebooks
young readers

Published by Sourcebooks Young Readers, an imprint of Sourcebooks Kids
P.O. Box 4410, Naperville, Illinois 60567-4410
(630) 961-3900
sourcebookskids.com

Library of Congress Cataloging-in-Publication Data

Names: Connolly, MarcyKate, author.
Title: Hollow dolls / MarcyKate Connolly.
Description: Naperville, Illinois : Sourcebooks Young Readers, [2020] |
    Sequel to: Comet rising. | Audience: Ages 8-14 | Audience: Grades 4-6
Identifiers: LCCN 2019024127 (print) | LCCN 2019024128 (ebook)
Subjects: CYAC: Magic--Fiction. | Families--Fiction. | Friendship--Fiction. | Fantasy.
Classification: LCC PZ7.1.C64685 Hol 2020  (print) | LCC PZ7.1.C64685
    (ebook) | DDC [Fic]--dc23
LC record available at https://lccn.loc.gov/2019024127
LC ebook record available at https://lccn.loc.gov/2019024128

This product conforms to all applicable CPSC and CPSIA standards.

Source of Production: Maple Press, York, Pennsylvania, United States
Date of Production: November 2019
Run Number: 5016686

Printed and bound in the United States of America.
MA 10 9 8 7 6 5 4 3 2 1

*For Mom and Dad*

# PROLOGUE

For as long as I can remember, I have served the Lady. I have always been hers to control, a pawn in every game she plays.

Today, that ends.

The shadow weaver, Emmeline, and her friends have caught my mistress here in her garden filled with giant flowers. I'm trapped, too, bands of the shadow that Emmeline controls holding me back.

I couldn't help the Lady even if I wanted to.

All I can do is watch as their talent taker strips Lady Aisling of her magic as punishment for her crimes. Then something extraordinary happens.

I'm freed. The invisible hold my mistress has had on my mind, that connection that forces my limbs to submit to her will, is broken. A strange, light feeling rises within me—hope, I think. Lady Aisling's wicked reign is finally over. I'm far from her only captive, and these rebel children with talents are our saviors.

Though the shadow weaver's bonds still hold me down, I feel as if I could float away. The Lady can't use me or my magic to harm people ever again.

My talent is mind reading. It's why Lady Aisling took me. Folks like me were blessed with magic when the Cerelia Comet flew by in the year of our birth, as it does every twenty-five years. There was a time when the comet-blessed were adored and revered, but that time is long past. Nowadays, people don't look as kindly on the talented as they once did. Many of the lucky ones who weren't captured by Lady Aisling have chosen to keep their talents hidden.

The comet came by in the year the Lady was born too. She is—was—a magic eater, someone who can steal another person's magic in order to wield it themselves. She used one of her stolen talents to create flowers out of other talented people, and she planted them here in her infamous Garden of Souls so that she could assume their powers just by nibbling on their petals. But something didn't quite work when she tried to transform the first of us with a mind-based talent—like me—into a flower. Still, she found a way to use us. I'll never forget the feeling of another mind crawling under my skin. Moving my arms and legs. Speaking with my voice.

But now I'm free. And I'm not alone.

The brilliant, beautiful garden Lady Aisling crafted from the souls of her magically talented prisoners unravels before my eyes. It's bizarre and beautiful at the same time. The air hisses with magic while flowers sprout heads, hands, and feet until they've returned to their original human form. Bewildered cries ring through the air, and underneath it all is the crush of many minds and their frantic thoughts. Nothing remains now of the flowers that I twirled past so many times—only barren dirt, dotted with hedges and grass. Nothing remains of the only life I can remember.

For the first time since I encountered the comet-blessed rebelling against the Lady, real fear creeps in. But so does hope.

Once it's determined that I and the other talented children Lady Aisling had under her control no longer pose a threat, we're released. The crowd of people in the garden swells every minute. Joyful reunions surround me. Parents and children, brothers and sisters, aunts and nephews and nieces.

But for many of us, no one comes. We begin to gather together in the middle of the garden, the confused and disoriented who aren't fully certain what happened or how. My best friend, Sebastian, finds me and squeezes my hand. Several of the Lady's other shells—those with mind-based talents who she used as puppets like me—join us. We're the lost souls of the Lady's garden, waiting for our past lives to find us.

But as the day marches on and night falls, our hopes begin to cool.

*Where are our families? What about* our *loved ones?* These thoughts circle me in a lazy loop.

But I'm not surprised. Only sad.

I pull a little sheet of paper from the pocket of my dirty white dress. I have several copies of this list, one always on my person, the others tucked away in different parts of my little cell inside the Lady's manor. If I lose one, I don't want to forget. On the paper is all that remains of my family. Four names and a location: Wren. Their faces are long lost; Lady Aisling's memory stealer took care of that. I cling to the paper, hoping against hope until the crowd begins to thin, leaving behind only those without families to claim us.

I slide the paper back into my pocket. I may have my freedom, but nothing more.

## TWO WEEKS LATER

When Lady Aisling's captives were freed, everyone eventually found their home. Relatives waiting for them. Some for weeks, months, years, even decades.

Waiting for everyone but me.

There is no trace left of my family because the village of Wren does not exist.

At least, that's what I've just been told.

The wind here in the garden where I sit—a very different, more modest one—tosses wisps of hair in my face, bringing me back to the conversation at hand.

"I'm sorry the network hasn't been able to figure out what happened to your family, Simone," Sebastian says, his curls twisting around the scar on his cheek like dark shadows. The network was formed in response to Lady Aisling's abduction of so many talented folks. The loved ones of the comet-blessed began to keep records and help each other evade the Lady's clutches. But that began long after I was taken.

Sebastian shifts uncomfortably on the bench. "Would you like to stay with mine?" His eye twitches. It does that sometimes. While the Lady no longer uses us, the effects of her magic linger. The people who freed us have yet to find a talent that can fix it. Without the Lady to give us a purpose, even one we hated, we're little more than hollow, broken dolls.

I tilt my head to gaze up at the white puffs of clouds, letting Sebastian's words make their way through my mind. Then I listen harder, waiting for the real meaning behind them.

*I know you can hear me—please say yes. Please say yes.*

I laugh and leap to my feet, suddenly fidgety. Staying too long in one place isn't good for me. Not until I find where I belong.

"Thank you. Yes." I like Sebastian's family. They've tried to help me locate my own family. His older sister, Jemma, is kind, and I can wander through the woods beyond their village whenever I please. Once she was only a couple years older than Sebastian. But the Lady held him captive for more than a decade, and now Jemma is all grown up and can be our guardian. One thing does give me pause though. "Your village is close to Lady Aisling's prison. I don't like that much." The village is in the territory of Parilla, just over the border from Abbacho. I'll stay with them for a while, but eventually I'll have to continue the search for Wren. I just don't have a clue yet where to start.

Sebastian's hand trembles on the garden bench. *I don't like that much either*, he thinks. "She can't trouble us anymore. We can pretend she doesn't even exist."

I know why Sebastian really wants me to remain here. He watched over me while we were under Lady Aisling's control in the Zinnian territory. He even took away the memories of the terrible things the Lady made me do. But he was acting out of guilt. His talent is memory stealing, and he's the one who took my memories of happier times in the first place.

I shiver, and Sebastian frowns.

"We'll keep searching, Simone. I promise."

I smile at him, but I don't think it comes off quite right, because he doesn't seem relieved.

"I know," I say. But I'm not sure there's anything left to find.

# CHAPTER ONE

Restless. That's how I feel every day. The need to wander and explore burns in my veins right alongside my blood.

This morning as I peer out the window of my little room, the sun shines on the woods behind Sebastian's village. I can never remember the name of it for long. He always reminds me, but then it slips away like dandelion puffs on a breeze. But the woods I adore. A maze of little streams wind between the trees, and I'm determined to follow every one of them to their destination before the end of summer.

My wandering helps me think through the problem of my

vanished family. It doesn't hurt that the woods happen to be on the side farthest from the Lady's prison.

"Simone?" Sebastian stands in my doorway, that look on his face again. The one he always gets when he has to call my name a few too many times. I climb off the bench by the windowsill sheepishly, as I feel the weight of his thoughts.

He's worried about me.

Many of Lady Aisling's other servants seem to be nearly their old selves again now that they're no longer under her spell. We've heard from old friends like Kalia the dream eater and Natasha the illusion crafter. They were nearly able to pick up their former lives where they left off. But not me. I'm not even sure what the old me was like.

Sebastian worries that I'm broken. It worries me too.

"Simone."

My eyes snap back to his, picking up the thread once again. "Good morning, Sebastian." I move toward him, momentarily distracted into a twirl. He puts his hands on my shoulders to stop me. I grin.

"My sister just received good news. There are people coming here tonight who might be able to help you."

I can't help peeking inside his mind. The words are a jumble—something about libraries—but I can feel excitement fizzing in every one.

"Who?"

"They're from the Parillan Archives. It holds historical records going all the way back as far as anyone can remember. If there's a trace of your village anywhere to be found, it will be there."

"The librarians are coming here?" My hands sway my skirts, even though I try to tell them not to.

Sebastian nods, and his mind begins to clear.

*They heard about Lady Aisling's garden and what happened to us.* "They want to interview us both in order to record the incident. That's what they wrote in their letter."

The swell of hope subsides. "Then they're not coming here to help me."

"But they might be able to all the same. We can ask."

I shrug, trying not to let my disappointment show too much.

"They'll be here tonight. Jemma wanted me to tell you to be sure you're home for dinner."

*And not muddy*, Sebastian can't help but think.

*I'll do my best*, I think back, sending my response into his mind, and he smiles.

Jemma gave up on making me useful weeks ago. I tried, but the tasks she gave me just couldn't hold my attention for long. There are too many minds, too many conversations, too many voices. It is loud and distracting, and I forget what I'm doing sometimes. The best she hopes for now is that I remember to come home after wandering in the woods or the village. At least I haven't forgotten that yet.

"I will, I promise."

"Are you going to the woods?" Sebastian asks, just as he does every day. I give the same answer too.

"Yes." I pause, already knowing what he's going to say next. "And I think I'd rather walk alone today."

He means well, but I go there to feel the quiet. Bringing him with me would defeat the purpose.

Sebastian and Jemma are kind to let me stay with them, but they are not quite mine. It doesn't help that I can hear their thoughts. Mind reading may sound like a wonderful talent—Lady Aisling certainly thought so—but the reality is less fun. In a village like this, full of people and lives and little red-roofed houses, all those minds are a constant dull roar. Sometimes when Sebastian is talking to me, I don't hear him over it at first. I have to work to block them out. Actual silence is a rare thing.

I slip out of the house, breezing by my friend, my head already full of silent leaves and babbling streams.

I trace the lines the streams make throughout the woods for hours until I finally sink onto the edge of a bank. The water doesn't think; it just gurgles and moves cheerily on its way. Every day is the same. There are no surprises for it, and even if there are, it simply flows around easily.

I am not water, though sometimes I wish I was.

I tuck my knees up to my chest and close my eyes, letting my magic reach out to my surroundings. Mind reading gives me a different sort of sight, almost like a new sense. I can feel any nearby minds. I've never measured the range, but the closer I am physically, the louder they are. There's a rabbit burrow nearby, hidden by a thicket, with a mother and three little ones. Mice and squirrels roam the underbrush, and every now and then the slippery thoughts of a silver fish swim past.

No one can sneak up on me, not even the curious rabbit poking her head out of the burrow. It's a young one, and I know that if I stay still, she'll come closer.

*It's all right, little one*, I tell her. It startles her back at first, but then she inches closer until she nudges my foot with her long whiskers. *May I pet you?* Rabbits don't have words. They think more in feelings and instinct, and hers are warm and welcoming. I reach out a tentative hand, all the while sending her reassuring thoughts. Her fur is soft, and she nuzzles up next to me.

As I pet her, my mind wanders. I don't have a lot of memories since Sebastian took them. It's like a thick, dull fog hovering in the back of my brain where those memories should be. But while I don't always remember the details of my service to the Lady, I do know that I'm responsible for expanding her garden, ferreting out those who tried to stay hidden while she crawled around under my skin. And even when she wasn't actively using me, I was still only half myself, trapped under the spells she used to keep her victims compliant. The thought makes me want to curl up in the hollow of one of these great trees and never leave.

Perhaps my family, my home, doesn't want to be found.

With any luck, the librarians coming to visit tonight will have answers. But what will I have to give in return? Reliving my time with the Lady is unpleasant. And tricky with all the gaps in my memories.

When the sun begins to flee the sky, I finally head back to Sebastian's home. The afternoon spent with the uncomplicated minds of squirrels and earthworms and the occasional curious fox and rabbit has smoothed the edges of my worries. I bid my new woodland friends goodbye and get to my feet, steeling my spine.

I retrace my steps slowly, letting my hands rove over the bark of the trees along the way and whisper over velvety ferns. Leaving the peace of the woods is never easy, but today it is especially hard. The route from the village gate to Sebastian's home takes me through the market square. Usually, there are so many people there that it's deafening, but no single mind ever stands out over the others, which makes it bearable for the few moments it takes to pass through.

Today is different.

The minute I set foot in the square, a sickly feeling washes over me, strong enough that I have to sit down in the middle of the street. It earns me more than a few stares.

*What's wrong with her?*

*Should I ask if she needs help?*

*Hmph. Lazy child.*

Icy hands seem to grip my throat as I scan the crowd. I don't see anyone out of place. But that awful feeling remains, a taint of magic lingering in the air.

I haven't felt this way since Lady Aisling used me as her shell. The feeling of some other mind roaming under my skin. I shudder.

The last thing I want to do is move toward it. But I must know the source. I have to be sure.

I scramble to my feet and push forward, following the feeling of that strange mind in the crowd. The noise rises as I get closer. My hands quake and twist in my skirts, but my feet keep moving of their own accord. When I press deeper into the mass of people, some minds scream louder than others. I do my best to push them away, but too many still get through.

*What is he doing?*

*Poor woman, Joe must have fallen and hit his head.*

I can't see much until I reach a break in the crowds. A man and woman argue by one of the stalls. On the surface, nothing much seems out of the ordinary. But the woman clutches the man's arm while he tries to shake her off. I have seen them before—they're a nice couple. The woman sells flowers, and the man fixes odds and ends for a price. Sometimes at the end of the day, she lets me have one of the flowers that are starting to wilt.

I go still and look closer at the pair, letting my talent loose. The woman's mind is frantic, but the man's is like hot coals.

*Help! Someone, help!*

I yank back my magic with a small cry. There are two minds in that man—the one the body belongs to, begging for help, and the dominant one, shoving the owner down.

My knees shake and I sink into the dirt, garnering even more odd looks for the second time that day. Jemma said it was best not to share my talent with the villagers. But they can still tell that there's something different about me.

The man continues to act strangely, and the cry of the

mind inside is too loud to bear. I manage to find my feet and then break into a run. I don't stop, don't listen to a single yell that follows me, until I'm free of the market crowds.

I know that talent all too well. Body walking. The ability to take control of another person's body and silence the mind inside. All it takes is one touch, and then the body walker can overtake a person whenever they want regardless of distance. The connection doesn't fade over time either. At any moment, a victim could be back under the body walker's command. No talent terrifies me more. Lady Aisling kept it in her garden. It's what she used to control me and Sebastian and her other servants.

But the original owner of that talent is no longer under the Lady's control. Now the body walker is on the loose.

# CHAPTER TWO

I halt in my tracks on the path to Sebastian's house. The Lady is imprisoned nearby. What if it isn't a body walker I witnessed but *her*, somehow free and up to her old tricks? My breath stutters, and I brace myself on the nearest tree.

I have to warn Sebastian. The Lady used him too. The thought of either of us being possessed again is more than I can stand. I break into a run so I don't lose my nerve.

As I enter Sebastian's little cottage, he is there to greet me.

"They're here," he says, his eyes alight with hope.

Fear tightens into a knot in my chest, and I grab his arm. "Sebastian, I need to tell you something—"

Jemma pokes her head into the hall. "Simone, we were

getting worried." She frowns, brushing her brown curly hair away from her face. The worry that had been gnawing at her begins to fade, and I can feel her irritation set in like an itchy cloak.

"I got distracted," I say, closing the door behind me.

*Again?* Jemma thinks. Then sheepishly turns away. She hasn't gotten used to having a mind reader around yet. Most people can go their whole lives without meeting someone with magic. And when they do, we take some getting used to.

"What do you want to tell me?" Sebastian asks, but Jemma clicks her tongue.

"That will have to wait until after dinner. We have guests, and it's rude to keep them waiting."

I swallow hard, trying to shove my racing heart back into place. Jemma steers me and Sebastian toward the table where the two librarians await us. One of them is a young woman with a curious mind who Jemma introduces as Rachel, while the older woman, Ida, looks me over as if I'm something to eat.

*What things these children must have seen… What they can do…*

I dutifully sit in my chair at the table while Jemma sets the food on our plates, but my toes tap the floorboards. If I can't warn them about the body walker soon, I might burst.

A sharp yank on my scalp snaps me out of it. My hair is tangled between my fingers. I must have pulled it myself.

The two librarians stare at me with muted fascination. I hold my magic back. I don't need to hear their thoughts to know what they think of me. It's clear as day on their faces.

I stick my hands under my legs to sit on them instead. Normally, I like Jemma's cooking, but today I don't think I could keep anything down.

"Thank you for hosting us," Ida says to Jemma. "We've been charged with recording the events surrounding Lady Aisling's garden, and we've heard many intriguing things. We're eager to hear their tales as well." She gestures to me and Sebastian.

Rachel's eyes sparkle. "We nearly had our own tale to tell on the way here. The next village over was having some trouble with what they believe was a shape shifter. We just missed them."

"Oh really?" Jemma puts some vegetables on each of our plates. "What kind of trouble?" There is a nervous tone to her voice that slips by our guests, but not me. Never me.

Ida waves her hand dismissively. "Nothing exciting. Just a mother not recognizing her own child. Classic shape shifter tomfoolery. The impostor ran off, and when they found the real mother, she could barely remember what had happened during the last few hours."

My spine goes rigid. That is too familiar, too close to what I witnessed this afternoon. I'd bet anything it was the body walker, not a shape shifter at all. Shape shifters mold their own bodies into different things, such as another person or an animal. If they copy someone's form, that person would never know unless they saw them with their own eyes. Body walkers are more dangerous. They take over a body, leaving the owner helpless and trapped inside until the body walker lets them have control again. This one must have come to our village afterward. I gulp in air, earning me a puzzled frown from Jemma.

"So, Sebastian, Simone, we understand you were both servants of Lady Aisling until her...imprisonment," Ida says.

I keep my eyes cast down, but Sebastian speaks up.

"Yes," he says. "But not willingly."

"Of course," Ida says. "Please tell us what you remember about your time with her." Rachel gets out a sheet of paper, but no quill. "From what we understand, many of her former servants do not remember much."

Sebastian turns a deep shade of red. Sadness pinches my

heart. We have talents that cut both ways. Sebastian might have been able to remove memories from others, but he is cursed to always keep his own.

Jemma puts down her fork. "Sebastian, you don't have to."

But he straightens up. "That's my fault," he says. "My talent is memory stealing. They don't remember because sometimes the Lady had me take their memories. Other times, they begged me to help them forget the things they'd done."

The librarians exchange a surprised glance. "Well, that certainly explains a lot." Rachel touches the page on her lap, and writing begins to appear upon it. With a start, I realize she's a book binder. Someone who can bind words to a page with their magic. From what I've heard, many of the old histories were written that way.

"What about you, Simone?" asks the younger librarian. "What is your talent?"

I stare at the food on my plate as if I'm willing it to disappear, just to have something to keep me grounded in this conversation. I have to stay focused and ask them for help. I can't let my mind wander off like it usually does.

"Mind reading."

Suddenly, they seem much more interested in me.

*Now* that *is a useful talent*, Rachel thinks.

My voice feels strange and gritty in my throat. I don't like the tenor of these people's thoughts. But one peek in Sebastian's direction keeps me rooted in my seat. His mind is full of infectious hope and possibility.

"I don't recall a lot about the times the Lady used me. Only snippets here and there. I know I was still in there somewhere when she controlled me. Just shoved down while her mind was in control." I shudder. "It was horrible."

Disappointment seeps across the table. "You don't recall anything interesting?" Ida asks. *What did Lady Aisling use these children for?*

I shrug, letting my fingers twist together into odd shapes in my lap. The awkward urge to laugh bubbles in my throat, but I choke it down.

"She often would send me with her hunters to find other talented children. I can sense minds. That was my role: to find anyone who was hiding." The words are hard to say, and even more uncomfortable to swallow. "Lord Tate was her main accomplice, until he had an accident. Then his nephew, Alden, took over."

The Lady's right-hand men were nearly as bad as she was. Thankfully, they were not talented, just ambitious. And they liked having us, or rather our talents, to give them an edge in the world.

"What about your everyday life? How did she treat you in Zinnia?"

Sebastian grabs my hand under the table.

"She kept us in small rooms on a lower level of her mansion until she needed our powers." Sebastian blinks rapidly. "It was practically a prison."

Except for me. I was her pet. I was allowed to wander, even when others were not. I could visit her garden anytime or explore the mansion. I don't know why I was special, but deep down in that part of my mind I don't like to visit, I have memories of specks of kindness from her.

"Terrible, though perhaps not quite as bad as others. Did you ever try to escape?" Ida's eyes have taken on a keen shine that I'm not sure I like. *I wonder if they even could…*

I shake my head, growing more uncomfortable by the second. "No, we were bespelled. She used the same spell on the parents of children she stole to prevent them from trying to rescue them."

The librarians' frustration balloons. They are almost done with their meal. I'm running out of time.

"Can you help me?" I blurt out, startling them.

"What do you mean?" Rachel says.

"The network has tried to find my family, but they can't locate them." I squeeze Sebastian's hand for encouragement. "We thought you might have a record of their village in your archives."

"What do you know about this village?" Ida asks.

"Only the name—Wren. It should be in Parilla. But no one has ever heard of it."

"It doesn't ring any bells," Ida muses. "We'd have to assign one of our librarians to pore over the archives, and we just don't have anyone to spare at the moment. All our librarians are currently assigned to other, more pressing tasks." She sits up straighter and folds her hands in her lap. "Unless, of course, there was some consideration to make this matter more urgent."

I want to cry out that it's urgent to me, but Jemma speaks first. Her expression has hardened. "You mean, if we pay you a fee."

Ida tilts her head. "We cannot abandon our other projects without the right motivation, you see." Rachel keeps her eyes cast down, and I peek inside her head before I can think better of it.

*Poor girl. We should help her.* Her eyes widen when she realizes I'm staring at her.

"You won't help a child who has had everything taken from her?" Jemma is on her feet now, her angry thoughts slipping from her mouth before her words. "Have you no compassion?"

Ida raises an eyebrow. "Of course we have compassion. But we also have needs that must be met. Our services must be paid for."

Jemma sighs. "And someone is funding this expedition of yours to find out more about Lady Aisling's garden, I suppose."

"Naturally."

"But that isn't fair!" Sebastian says. Jemma hushes him. Disappointment crawls through my veins, weighing me down.

"I think it's time for you to leave," Jemma says.

"I see," Ida says, rising. "Thank you for the meal and for sharing your stories. It is most appreciated." With that, she sweeps out of the room. Rachel follows close behind, but not without an apologetic glance in my direction.

"I'm sorry, Simone," Jemma says, sinking into her chair. "I thought they'd be more open to helping. I should have known better than to get your hopes up."

"What now?" Sebastian says.

My reason for arriving late to dinner bursts back to the forefront of my mind. I grab his arm. "I must tell you something important." My voice feels hoarse and thin. "Remember how the Lady controlled us? How she must have been using a body walker's talent?"

Sebastian goes rigid, and Jemma straightens up, listening more attentively.

"Now that her garden is gone, the owner of that talent is free. And"—I swallow hard, twisting my hair around my fingers with my free hand—"they were here. Today in the market, I felt them. I could hear the screams of the mind whose body they stole begging for help." I examine my muddy shoes. "I fled. I couldn't stand to be there a second longer. I can't experience that again."

Sebastian begins to shake, and Jemma pulls him to her side, wrapping an arm around him. Her expression softens, as do her thoughts.

"You're both safe now. You're protected. And we'll find some other way to locate your family, Simone."

*But who will protect me if someone comes after them?* she thinks.

If Lady Aisling had anything to do with this, we're all in grave danger, talented or not.

I shake my head, wisps of my pale hair waving across my face. "The body walker was using people. And that shape shifter the librarians mentioned? That must have been the body walker too. Either that, or the Lady isn't as powerless as we've been told. We're not safe." I begin to pace erratically. "I should leave."

Sebastian's face falls. "But why? Where will you go?"

"I need to see Lady Aisling," I say. Sebastian recoils, and the force of his objection almost knocks me over. I steady myself against the wall. "It's the only way to know for sure that she really is powerless now."

"Please stay, Simone." *Please don't leave me alone. You're the only one who understands.*

Jemma straightens up. "You know that's not necessary, Simone. That talent taker, Noah, removed her magic for good. Besides, she's in a prison, being guarded night and day. If she had her powers back, someone would know."

Sebastian doesn't say anything, but his thoughts are a mess of swirling fear.

"The guards can't see into her mind. If her powers are

back, if she's somehow got any trace of the talents she stole, I have to know." My whole body begins to shake. "I won't be able to sleep again until I'm sure."

This time, Jemma puts an arm around me, too, and I lean into the warmth of her kind thoughts. "All right. But you're not going alone. We'll all go together."

# CHAPTER THREE

I do not sleep much at all. Sebastian's anxious thoughts in the next room keep me up. His sister may be sure that our former mistress is no longer a threat, although Sebastian and I don't feel as confident.

But when the sun crawls over the sky, I let my talent stretch for a few moments just to feel the stirrings of minds in the village. Soft echoes of dreams bounce through my head, painting strange pictures. Sometimes, when the Lady wasn't actively using me, I'd sneak away and wander for a while. The garden looked lovely, but was loud. All those minds trapped and confused, and too many that had lost all hope. It was enchanting on the outside, but a nightmare underneath.

I squeeze my eyes closed, trying to shut out these thoughts.

I sit up straight in bed. My fitful dreams last night have only made me more determined to see Lady Aisling for myself. The need prickles under my skin. It won't go away until I know for certain that she can't hurt us ever again.

But there's something else I must ask her. She's the only one left who might know where I came from.

I throw off the covers and slip out of my room to wake Sebastian. The sooner we can leave, the better.

An hour later, we're loading the family carriage. It's a carved wooden and metal contraption, similar to the ones Lady Aisling owned, but not as extravagant. It's simpler, and I like it all the better for it.

The horse leading the carriage, Red, huffs as we approach. *Hello.* I place a hand on her soft mane. *Thank you for taking us.*

She huffs again and nuzzles my hand. I pull an apple out of my bag and let her eat it. Her approval surrounds me like a warm blanket.

"Come on, Simone," Jemma says. She and Sebastian are already settled, Sebastian in the back of the carriage and Jemma on the driver's box. Sebastian's family is not rich; they have a few comforts like this carriage, but not enough money to pay a driver. Fortunately, Jemma is an excellent horsewoman. I've seen her taking Red out to the fields near the village many a morning.

I climb up after Sebastian, and we leave the village behind. I sit up on my knees, watching it get farther and farther away. With every beat of the horse's hooves, the tightness in my chest unwinds.

The drive is only a couple of miles, but it feels like an eternity. The closer we get to the Lady, the more anxiety I feel rise in Sebastian like a tide. I squeeze his hand encouragingly. It only helps a little. But a little is better than nothing.

I doze off for a bit, and when I open my eyes, we've stopped in front of a hulking stone building. It is all sharp angles and lines, with no hint of softness about it.

I like it very much. As long as her powers are gone, this should hold the Lady well.

But as I step down from the carriage, my legs feel weak and wobbly, and I unconsciously tug my power back. Part of me is terrified to accidentally touch the Lady's mind even if she is behind bars.

Jemma grips our hands and takes us into the prison after speaking to the guard outside. He appraises us with raised eyebrows. Another guard leads us down a stone hallway that feels as cold as a tomb. Little by little, I let my talent explore, touching on the minds hidden behind the doors and walls. This building contains more rage and despair than I have ever seen. And evil. It lurks around every corner. I shiver and pull my cloak close. Sebastian squeezes my hand, and I squeeze back.

The guard stops in front of a triple-locked door, and his keys jangle as he opens it. The door swings wide, but Sebastian balks when the guard gestures for us to enter. Jemma glances back and forth between the two of us, uncertain what to do.

"You don't have to, Sebastian," I say. His relief is palpable.

*Thank you*, he thinks. I duck into the room. Inside there is a narrow walkway between the wall and a row of bars keeping the prisoner secured in the tiny room. In the center, an ancient woman sits on a chair with a ratty blanket wrapped around her shoulders.

She looks nothing like the beautiful young woman who held us captive, but the shape of her mind is as sharp and cruel as ever. When I meet her milky eyes, she sits up on the edge of her seat.

"My pet?" she says. Gone is the familiar lilt to her voice. Was it magic or real? I'll probably never know for certain. Now the edges are rough, but as commanding as ever. I can't help but cringe, though I try to stay strong. I clasp my shaking hands together behind my back.

"I am not yours."

She cackles, the lines on her face wrinkling deeper. "You will always be mine, Simone."

"Is it true?" I say. I can barely find the words, and I fear if I peer too deeply into her, I may never escape.

She tilts her head. "What? Have I really lost my talent? Do you think that I choose to remain here?" The Lady scoffs, then shuffles toward the bars. I take a step back, and my fingertips meet the cold stone wall. "Well, take a peek. See for yourself."

Something about her is different, aside from her appearance. The magic bubbling beneath the surface seems to be gone. "Where did you steal me from? I need to know."

The Lady laughs. "You've grown bold, my dear. Coming here and making demands."

"Please." I step forward, my hair floating around me like a living thing.

"Poor child. Sebastian took a few too many of your memories, didn't he?" She shakes her head. "Does he remember it? Does he regret it?"

A wicked gleam shines in her eyes, and something uncomfortable forms in the pit of my stomach. "What do you mean? Of course he does."

She laughs. A horrid, coarse sound, until she begins to cough and has to sit down again. I can stand it no longer. I have to look. I need what I came for.

I close my eyes, leaning against the wall for support, and let my mind explore hers. She has walls built up. She knows my talent, having used it for so long. But I can feel the terrible sense of loss that pervades every thought—her talent is truly gone. She feels it like one would a lost limb. And she's furious that she's too weak to do anything about it.

I open my eyes and realize she's staring directly at me with a horrible expression on her face.

*Sebastian didn't take your memories—it was me. You were the first I used to experiment with his talent.*

I recoil.

"Your memories of home were holding you back. I removed them. And then you were perfect. A model servant."

"A slave, you mean," I hiss. Poor Sebastian. He's blamed himself that I can't remember my parents, but it was Lady Aisling controlling him with the body walking talent. Of course it was. Perhaps that was why I wrote those names down on paper. I must have suspected what she was going to do. "Where did you find me? What happened to my family?"

She shrugs. "You were my first servant. It was a long time ago, and with this old mind, I can hardly remember a thing."

A glimpse into her head convinces me she's telling the truth. She kept me and the rest of her servants alive for so long using the talent of a life bringer, just as she did herself. And she used a youth keeper's magic to ensure our minds and bodies remained young and easy to control. Even removing my memories helped, because it doesn't feel to me like I've lived that long at all. But there is something else I can't grab on to. Something she's hiding, even from me.

Perhaps I can at least get something about the body walker from her. A name or a description would be a start.

"You had a body walker in your garden. Who was it? What was their name?"

Lady Aisling smiles, revealing crooked teeth and bright gums.

*If you ever find out, you'll regret it.*

# CHAPTER FOUR

The force of Lady Aisling's thought hits me like a slap to the face. I flee the cell and don't breathe again until the door is locked behind me.

"Simone!" Sebastian's warm hand on my back steadies me. The Lady's words still ring in my ears. *You'll regret it…*

Regret what? And why?

I shiver and someone puts a blanket over my shoulders. The buzz of confusion from other minds rings in my ears, and I squeeze my eyes shut. My hold on my talent is not as tight as it once was. Someone leads me out of the suffocating stone prison—Sebastian, I think—and when I feel the warm air on my face, I open my eyes and breathe in deeply.

Sebastian stands next to me shifting from foot to foot, Jemma behind him with a steady hand on his shoulders. "What did she say?" he asks.

"Nothing good." I clench and unclench my hands. "She wouldn't say anything about my family and village—or even the body walker—only that I'll regret it if I find out more about them."

"That sounds like a threat," Jemma says, nervously glancing back at the prison. "We should go. There's an inn and tavern not far from here where we can have a bite for lunch. Food would do you both good, I think."

She ushers us back to the carriage, her expression growing more determined with every step. "I've been thinking, Simone," she says. "We can't let Lady Aisling win. There must be some trace of your village somewhere." She halts in front of the carriage and faces us both. "What do you think about going to the Parillan Archives ourselves? I know those librarians yesterday were unbearable, but if we plead our case to the head librarian to let us do our own research there, I don't know how they could turn us away."

A small spark of hope lights in my chest, but I'm almost afraid to give it air. "Do you really think they'll let us?"

"Simone, you're the last of Lady Aisling's captives. Everyone else found their homes, but your past is still a mystery. At the very least, they should be intrigued. And if we do the work ourselves, all they have to do is give us access. We can even offer to do dishes or other labor around the library to earn our keep, if necessary."

Sebastian's eyes are bright. "It's worth a try."

I nod. "All right. Let's go to the Archives."

We get into the carriage, Jemma and Sebastian buoyed up by the new plan. But I'm too afraid to let myself hope. I look back once more at the prison and shudder as we drive away. Lady Aisling is hiding something. Something important about my past. That can't spell anything good for us.

When we reach the inn, Jemma settles us at one end of a long wooden table in the tavern with steaming bowls of beef stew.

"I'm just going to settle with the innkeeper and check on our horse. I'll be back in a few minutes." She hurries off.

There are all sorts of curious minds here. Men and women

from across the three territories, every one with a story to tell. Once, I would have let them all flood in—that's what the Lady preferred in order to spy as thoroughly as possible—but now I do my best to hold back the torrent.

My grip on my magic is looser than it should be, and I need to practice more. But it's exhausting and easier to simply be alone. I don't have that luxury right now, and by the time we're midway through our meals, I'm nearly worn out from the effort.

Sebastian wipes his mouth on a napkin and pushes his bowl aside. "At least the Lady really is powerless," he says. "That's good news."

He's grasping at anything to keep himself from succumbing to fear of the body walker. I try to smile.

"It is. But the other things she said were strange. And didn't really make a lot of sense. I don't understand why she thinks I'll be sorry if I ever find out who the body walker is."

Sebastian shudders involuntarily. "Maybe just that it would mean you have to get too close to them to get away."

An uncomfortable feeling swims through my belly. Sebastian might be on to something. "And that would mean that I could be used by them like she used us."

"That would definitely be something to regret."

I push a piece of potato around my bowl. There's something else I must tell Sebastian, but I hope this will be good news for him, not troubling.

"The Lady said something about you while I was there."

Sebastian freezes, every muscle tensing. I place a hand on his arm.

"Don't worry, it isn't bad. *She* took the memories of my past, not you."

He frowns. "What do you mean?"

"When she captured you, she used your talent to remove years of my life. She said it was holding me back. You only willingly took the memories I asked you to, bad ones from missions she made me go on. It isn't your fault I can't remember my family."

Sebastian's face brightens as relief floods his thoughts. I don't think I ever realized how guilty he felt about that until now. "I always thought I'd messed up. Taken too many by accident when you'd asked me to help you."

His happiness makes me smile. "No, it was all her." I finish the last of my lunch and set my bowl aside. "Shouldn't your sister be back by now?" I frown, reaching out for Jemma's mind.

My heart skips a beat when I don't feel her thoughts nearby.

"Maybe the innkeeper's busy. There are lots of people here this afternoon," Sebastian says. He glances at me, and his face pales. "What's wrong, Simone?"

My hands twist, and my knee bounces under the table. "Probably nothing. But I can't hear her thoughts."

Sebastian gets to his feet. "What?" The other travelers having their meals begin to stare. But I don't care, and neither does Sebastian. The same fierce terror runs through us. I try to calm us both down.

"She must have gone across the street. Somewhere out of range. Maybe she's down by the stables. She did say she was going to check on the horse. Maybe it's farther than we thought." The words pour from my mouth as we hurry in the direction we last saw Jemma go.

*Poor kids.*

*Those urchins better not try to steal my bags.*

*Didn't anyone teach them not to run inside?*

I do my best to shut out the travelers' thoughts until we finally get outside. The afternoon is warm and bright, but not soothing. We follow the cobblestone path lined by tall grass and trees down to the stables. A gentleman walks toward the inn, barely giving us a glance as he passes. But I reach inside his head, just to see. His only thoughts are of how hungry he is and how annoyed he is at his horse. I let out a breath, relieved.

When we near the stables, I send my magic inside, but all I find are the minds of animals, including Red, all sleepy and content. Except for one who is just as annoyed at his owner for running him ragged. A stable hand dozes somewhere in the building as well.

I grab Sebastian's hand. "She isn't there."

His eyes are wide and watery. "Simone, where would she go? She wouldn't just leave us, would she?"

I think back to all the times I've accidentally slipped into Jemma's mind. While the responsibility for two new children was unexpected for her—especially after her brother had been missing for more than a decade—it was not unwelcome. She loves Sebastian, and she's kind to me. She wouldn't abandon us.

"No, she'd never."

Sebastian's growing panic leaches into my head. It winds around our throats, threatening to choke us both.

"Come on." I tug Sebastian back toward the inn, and once inside, we head directly up the stairs toward the rooms instead of back to the tavern area. It's the only place we haven't searched yet, though I can't imagine why she'd be there. The hallway is dark and shadowed, but no mind can hide from me. We start down the hall, my magic reaching into every corner, until I finally alight on something familiar, but it slips away before I can read it clearly.

"This way," I say. We round a corner, and Sebastian cries out. A shape that looks like Jemma's stands at the end of the hall, trying to unlock the door to a room. I freeze.

Something's wrong.

"Jemma!" Sebastian cries, and the figure's head jerks up. "Where have you been?"

My hands begin to twitch. I can't feel Jemma's mind, even though her body stands before us, slack-jawed with surprise. Another consciousness controls her instead. My breath grows short.

"I don't have time for this." She shoves past Sebastian as if she doesn't even know him, and he falls to the floor.

I flatten against the wall, squeezing my eyes shut as Jemma hurries past me too. As she does, the sickening feel of the mind of the body walker in our guardian's body makes my knees tremble.

The dominant thoughts are singularly focused: *I must find them. I must find them.*

But the body walker doesn't seem to know what "them" is, only a vague idea that something is missing and must be found.

I scramble to my feet and shakily help Sebastian to his. *It's the body walker*, I tell him.

Sebastian's lip trembles. "We have to do something." He shakes off my hand and runs after his sister and the mind that controls her.

For a moment, terror freezes me in place. The thought of going anywhere near the body walker is enough to make me nauseous. But I can't leave Sebastian alone. And I can't let him do something foolish.

I catch up to him as he corners his sister on the stairwell. His despair is as thick as smoke.

"Jemma, it's me. Please!"

I grab his shoulder and yank him back. His satchel slips down his arm. "It's not her anymore, Sebastian. It's not her. She doesn't know us."

Jemma brushes off her sleeve with a shrewd light in her eyes. "What makes you think that, girl?"

"Nothing. I don't know anything." I shudder and pull Sebastian down the stairs, but Jemma grabs hold of his arm.

"Oh, I think you do. You have a talent, don't you?" Jemma grins in such an un-Jemma-like fashion that it's downright chilling.

I send my thoughts as loud as I can into Sebastian's muddled head, hoping he hears me over the confusion roaring in his brain.

*The body walker knows. Somehow they know we're talented!*

That gets Sebastian moving again. He jerks backward, stumbling into me as Jemma lunges for us. We run down the hall away from her, but in the wrong direction. She's right behind us, blocking our path to the stairs.

"Now, what talents do you have? Let me guess. Something mind-based? Something that allowed you to know I'm not the woman you thought I was?"

I risk a glance back, only to find a look of twisted glee on Jemma's face. Panic shoots through me, and we duck into the nearest room.

Sebastian spins around, panicking. *What do we do? Where do we go now?*

I rush to the window, but the drop down is too far. We'd never make it in one piece. I swallow hard and steel my spine.

We have to face her down. We have no other choice.

The door creaks open, and Sebastian and I clasp hands tightly. We back up instinctively as Jemma appears in the doorway, an unnatural smile on her face.

"Now, why don't you just make it easy on us all and come here?" She holds out her hands as if she actually believes we will take them.

*Take the memory of meeting us, and let's go. Just make sure you take it from the body walker's mind and not your sister's.*

Sebastian goes rigid. He steps forward and grips Jemma's hand. She jerks him closer.

"Now, what can you do? Tell me…" Her eyes go blank, then she blinks rapidly for a moment, confused. She releases Sebastian, staring at him as if she's never seen him before.

I know I only have a few moments, but I concentrate with everything I've got, until I finally hear Jemma's thoughts faintly crying out.

*Run! Simone, take Sebastian and run! I'll meet you at the Archives, I promise.*

Jemma's expression changes from surprise to irritation, so different from the desperation I just heard.

*Run!* I think-shout to Sebastian. *Jemma wants us to run!* We escape down the stairs and burst through the inn's front door, the yelp of the innkeeper we nearly bowled over following us into the street.

Tears stream over Sebastian's cheeks and stain mine as well. We duck behind a large oak tree in the yard, out of view of the inn's windows, to catch our breath.

"What are we going to do now?" Sebastian says between sobs. *My only family, my only family...* His thoughts circle.

"We need to put as much distance between us and that body walker as possible." The understanding of what that means brings fresh tears to both our eyes. It means leaving Jemma behind. Or risking becoming victims again. Enslaved again.

Nothing terrifies us more.

"It's what Jemma wants," I say. "Just before we ran, she said to go to the Archives and she'll meet us there."

Sebastian agrees, even though leaving his sister behind is like leaving one of his limbs. He wraps his arms around his middle as if trying to hold himself together.

"The body walker won't control her forever. They'll have to become bored with it at some point or at least sleep and let her go. Then Jemma will be free of their power. We'll wait for her at the Archives, and if she doesn't show up, maybe we can contact someone in the network that freed us from Lady Aisling to help."

A grain of hope lodges in Sebastian's brain, softening his thoughts.

"The Parillan librarians might know how to help too. Maybe they'll have something on how to force a body walker out." I say, warming up to the idea even as the words leave my mouth. "And we at least have an idea where the Archives are."

I thread my arm through Sebastian's, and together we enter the forest, wide-eyed. He quakes next to me, sometimes tripping over his feet. Though my chin trembles, I send reassuring thoughts his way. I can feel the minds of every animal nearby—curious, hungry, sleeping—and not one of them is threatening. We'll be safe enough for now.

But tomorrow there are no guarantees.

# CHAPTER FIVE

We hurry through the woods, hoping to come across a footpath or road. But as the day goes on, all we find are trees, bushes, and hills for what feels like miles. We may even be walking in circles. We're both exhausted, and I'm finding it especially hard to focus. Everything looks like more of the same.

When we hear what sounds like someone moaning, we're both startled to a stop.

*Could it be the body walker?* Sebastian thinks, his hands quivering.

The moan comes again. I frown. *How could they have*

*gotten all the way out here? And why would they be moaning? Let's just take a peek. It could be someone alone and hurt.*

Sebastian swallows hard.

*What if that's how a body walker sounds when they use their talent? We know they don't have to be near their victims to control them. They just have to touch them once, and that's it.*

*Then why didn't Lady Aisling ever sound like that when she was controlling us?*

That finally makes Sebastian's thoughts calm. *That's true. She never did act like that.*

We tiptoe toward the sound, moving as quietly as we can through the bushes. The noise gets louder as we approach, until the rustling and moaning is just up ahead. My palms sweat, and I try to smile encouragingly at Sebastian, but it comes off as a grimace.

*Just a few more steps,* I think at him. With my heart in my throat, I part the bushes. In the clearing ahead sits a man curled into the fetal position and holding his head in his hands.

Frowning, I peek into his mind.

*Where am I? What happened?*

The same thoughts chase each other through his head over and over. I tiptoe back to where Sebastian waits.

*It's just a man. He seems to be lost.* I shrug. *Maybe he fell off his horse?*

*That's all?* Sebastian thinks. *Is he hurt?*

*There's no blood, and I couldn't see so much as a bruise on him. His thoughts don't show him to be in pain either.* Pain tends to be an all-consuming sort of thing. Whenever I'm near someone who's hurt, it feels as if they're shouting in my ears. It's almost as painful for me as it is for them.

Sebastian begins to shake. *But what if someone hurt him? What if they're still around?*

I place my hands on my friend's shoulders and close my eyes, searching for any hint of another human mind nearby. *No one else is here. I'd sense their thoughts if they were.*

He begins to relax a little. *We should still get out of here quickly. Just in case they come back.*

I glance back at the man in the clearing. He's managed to get to his feet and is stumbling around. I know Sebastian is right, but part of me wishes to help the man. We don't know him, and we can't rule out that it might be some sort of trick meant to trap us. His thoughts do seem sincerely confused, but there's something off about the whole thing that I can't quite put my finger on.

Still, I don't feel right just leaving him here.

*I'm going to try to talk to him. It'll only take a minute.*

*Simone, no!*

I turn back toward the clearing, this time stepping out from the bushes. The man shrinks back.

"Who…who are you?" His voice quavers. He holds out his hands and stares at them, then back at me. "Who am I?"

I can sense Sebastian hiding in the bushes behind me, but he doesn't dare reveal himself.

"I'm Simone. But I don't know who you are. We—I heard you from the path. Are you all right?"

"Where are we?" He steps closer, though he is still unsteady on his feet.

I frown. "I'm not really sure, actually. Somewhere in Parilla. There's a tavern and inn somewhere around here…" I let my voice trail off, realizing I must sound very unhelpful. I don't wish to confuse him even more.

I risk a quick glance back toward Sebastian, when suddenly the man lurches forward and grabs me by the shoulders.

"What happened? Where am I? Tell me! Tell me, please!"

I struggle, but his grip is much more solid than his feet.

Desperation consumes the man's thoughts with questions I can't answer.

"Let her go!" Sebastian bolts out of the bushes swinging his pack. It startles the man enough to loosen his grasp so I can break free. Sebastian grabs my hand, and we dart back into the bushes, running as though our lives depend on it.

*I told you it was dangerous to talk to him!*

I shudder. While I'm not sure the man himself is dangerous, clearly something bad happened to him. I don't want to stick around long enough for it to happen to us too.

Together, we head back toward the path. It's safer for us to remain in the woods, hidden from other people, until we reach somewhere public, like a village with lots of places to hide—or even better, our destination, the Parillan Archives.

Suddenly, my foot catches on something, and I go flying into the ferns. The breath is knocked from my lungs. For a moment, I sit there, just as dazed as the man in the clearing.

Sebastian helps me up, and I brush off my dress. He attempts to make a joke but still can't muster a smile. "What have I told you about daydreaming?"

I manage to laugh, though my ribs feel a bit sore. "Not

to do it while I'm walking." The hem of my dress is torn and smudged with green and brown. "At least the ferns were soft."

He yawns. "Do you think we'll find another town before nightfall?"

I shake my head. "I doubt it. We'll probably have to sleep in the woods tonight." If we were near a village, I'd sense it by now.

Sebastian looks stricken. I'd almost forgotten how much he hates sleeping outside. Back when we were the Lady's, he'd had no choice when she sent him on missions. When he returned, he was always exhausted because he could barely sleep for fear of all the things that lurked in the darkness.

But I'm not afraid. Once, the Lady used me to talk down a bear while we were on an excursion for her. Convinced it to walk right out of the camp and away from our food stores. It was terrifying while it was happening, but now I know it can be done. And I could do it again if I had to. Well, as long as I got some sleep first.

"Let's keep walking, and we'll see what we can find." We continue on, our steps getting more and more lethargic.

Darkness begins to descend, and with it come new sights and sounds. Fireflies flickering between the trees like stars come down to earth. The chirp of crickets, rustling under brush, and the occasional hoot of an owl that makes Sebastian jump. He got the scar across his cheek from an owl a few months ago. It's a shame the Lady didn't have a chance to use a healing talent on it before she lost her powers.

We keep moving until we reach another clearing—this one without any strange, confused men. We can move no farther tonight. We manage to use our cloaks from our packs as bedrolls, and then collapse upon them, side by side, under the night sky.

Sebastian tosses and turns until I fill his head with thoughts of the warmth and safety of a locked house and roaring fire. Soon his breathing evens out into a steady rhythm, and I let slumber carry me away too.

## CHAPTER SIX

When we wake the next morning with leaves in our hair and aches in our necks, nothing looks familiar. The trees are the same, and so are the soft, trundling minds of the small animals going about their morning. But there is no path anymore, no clear way forward. I can't even tell which direction we came from last night.

We're lost.

My stomach rumbles loudly, and Sebastian glances at me. We haven't eaten anything since lunch at the tavern yesterday.

*I'm scared*, he thinks.

I am, too, but telling him that won't help. The manic urge to just *run*, headlong and without heeding direction, fills me, but I manage to keep my feet in place.

"I guess we didn't plan very well," I say, trying to keep my voice light. It cracks anyway, and Sebastian flinches.

"There has to be a village around here somewhere, doesn't there?" he asks.

I shrug. "I hope so." Fear gnaws at my stomach, spurring me to put together our meager belongings and get moving.

As we walk, I think back to the times I traveled with the Lady's men. Did they ever pass through here? Did I ever see them eating berries or leaves? I scan the underbrush for anything that looks like it might possibly be edible, but all I find are dried leaves, ferns, and broken branches. The lone good thing about the Lady was that she always kept her servants well fed. We would've been useless to her otherwise.

The day drones on, and our hunger becomes a sharp, pointed thing. By late afternoon, my legs wobble as we wind between trees. The forest is beautiful, and I might love this place if it wasn't terrifying to be far from everything I know.

I spy a squirrel scampering through the leaves, and an idea

strikes me. I grab Sebastian's arm but don't say a word for fear of scaring away the animal.

*The animals are hungry too. Let's follow them. They know where they're going.*

Sebastian smiles for the first time since we fled the body walker.

We creep after the squirrel, and I keep the threads of my magic hooked into the little animal's mind. Calm thoughts fill the connection between us, some of my own hunger no doubt creeping in too. Soon the squirrel feels safe with us follow-ing close behind, and we no longer need to work hard not to scare him. The forest begins to thin, but the squirrel knows his path. Soon we hit a break in the trees, and the woods open up into fields for miles with a little village overlooking them on a hill.

The field directly in front of us contains an apple orchard.

Sebastian and I grin, and the squirrel squeaks. Then he launches forward through the tall grass.

We waste no time doing the same.

We scoop apples into my satchel, then huddle under the largest tree and eat our way through the spoils. The apples are crunchy and sweet, and I don't care a whit that juice runs down my chin. It's the most delicious thing I've ever tasted.

"That was brilliant," Sebastian says. But as our hunger fades, the fear creeps back into his thoughts. "What do you think the body walker wanted with my sister?"

My hands twist the stem off an apple. "I don't know. I'm sorry, Sebastian." I thought the talented folks who were freed would all be good and happy to be human again. Everyone else found their families, after all. It never occurred to me until now that some of them might be just as bad as Lady Aisling herself. I shudder, and Sebastian sucks his breath in sharply as a wave of panic rolls over him.

That's when we hear the dogs.

First the barks, then as they get closer, their singular thoughts buzz in my head: *thieves, thieves, thieves…*

I scramble to my feet, dragging Sebastian with me. Frantically, I glance around but find no easy hiding place.

The woods it is.

*Run*, I think to Sebastian, and we take off into the forest, just as the dogs reach the orchard. Hoofbeats pound after them, no doubt the owner of this orchard, unhappy that we've trespassed.

We have no good excuse to make, no money to pay for what we've eaten. Flight is the only option.

Our feet are tired, and we stumble often. Soon our legs and arms are covered in cuts and scratches. But we dare not stop. We don't even notice the direction we run, we just keep moving, terror filling every single thought.

We don't see the shack until we're nearly on top of it.

We skid to a halt, our already short breaths stuttering in our chests. The roof is lopsided, and the wood holding the structure up looks as though it could topple any second.

But it's also the only place we have to hide. The dogs' sharp barks still echo through woods after us. We don't have much time.

We creak open the door, hearts thudding in our ears. Only when we close the door behind us do we take in the room.

I let out a squeal of surprise, and so does Sebastian. I clamp my hand over my mouth, and we huddle together.

A woman sits at a small wooden table in the corner of the room, eating a meal of bread and cheese. Our surprise is mirrored in her eyes.

"Who are you?" she asks.

Sebastian glances at me wild-eyed and uncertain. I peek into the woman's mind and find she isn't angry, but genuinely curious. Even a little worried about us, given the state we're in.

My shoulders relax, and I squeeze Sebastian's hand.

"I'm Simone, and this is Sebastian. I'm sorry we intruded on your home. We needed a place to hide."

The woman stands, her meal forgotten. She is tall and auburn-haired with gray eyes, keen as a cat's.

*Poor dears. They remind me of my own children…*

I pull my magic out of her head. While I'm curious, it seems rude to read her mind since we just barged into her house and need her help. I'm encouraged that her thoughts have a kind bent and that she doesn't seem the least put off by Sebastian's scar.

"You can call me Maeve. What are you hiding from? You look as though you've seen a ghost, or two at least."

After what we've been through, we just aren't built to trust strange women. But this one seems kind.

Sebastian stares at his toes. "We were starving. We happened upon an apple orchard and took some to eat." His words are punctuated by the howls of the dogs closing in on us.

"I see. They're after you then." Maeve suddenly lights up. "Well, we can't just let them have you, now can we? Come, there must be somewhere for you to hide around here while I get rid of them." She gets up and pokes around the house and soon discovers a crawl space under the stairs. "Here we go." She gestures for us to follow, but we both hesitate for a moment.

*She can't be worse than the dogs*, I think to Sebastian.

*Or the dogs' owners*, he thinks back.

We follow and curl up together under the stairs. Panic flits over us as the door closes, leaving us in the dark. But I close my eyes and remind myself—and Sebastian—that this is only temporary. Maeve wants to help. Besides, she has no way of knowing we're talented and no reason to want to use us like Lady Aisling did.

We hear the front door of the shack open and close, and the sound of the dogs barking up to the front door.

"Have you seen two small thieves hereabouts?" shouts the angry voice of a man. "Our dogs are certain they're nearby."

"I'm afraid I'm alone. Haven't seen anyone," Maeve says. "The only thing your dogs smell here is my lunch. Here, they can have some of it. Roasted chicken."

The man growls as the dogs stop barking, no doubt eating the offered food.

"Fool beasts, thinking with their bellies. What good are the lot of you?" He continues to berate his animals as they depart.

As the sounds of the dogs and horses fade, my hopes rise. We're safe, and we've found help. Perhaps we'll make it through this journey in one piece after all.

# CHAPTER SEVEN

A few moments later, Maeve comes back inside and opens the door under the stairs. The light in the house is starting to fade as the sun sets.

"They're gone. You should be safe now."

A laugh bubbles in my throat, but I choke it down and only a little squeal comes out. I don't wish for this kind woman to think I'm odd.

"Thank you," Sebastian says.

Maeve places her hands on her hips and stares at us. "Now what am I going to do with you two?" She looks so serious for a moment that I cringe, but then she breaks into a laugh. "I have just the thing." She opens a bag next to her chair and pulls out more food, including some of the chicken she used to drive away the dogs. "Eat. I know you're hungry. You don't seem like the sort to go stealing apples for fun."

She gestures to the other chairs by the table, and Sebastian and I don't hesitate. Maeve watches us while we eat, and I can't help it. My grip on my talent slips, and her thoughts open to me again.

*A boy and a girl, just like my children...*

I glance away, seeing the melancholy shine in her eyes. She must have lost her children. Just like we lost our parents. What an awful thing. All of us, missing little pieces of our lives.

Maeve straightens up and smooths her skirts. "So, where are you two headed? And where is your family?"

I realize she must assume we're brother and sister. "Oh, we're not related. I'm"—I pause, considering how much to tell her—"an orphan. And I've been staying with Sebastian's family. We're headed to the Parillan Archives to see if we can locate any of my relatives."

*Let's not tell her about our talents just yet,* I think to Sebastian. *Good idea.*

"And what about Sebastian's family? Aren't they traveling with you?"

"Well, they were." My hands twist uncomfortably in my lap.

"We got separated," Sebastian says. "My older sister is our guardian, and we don't know where she is now."

"But"—I glance at Sebastian—"she's supposed to meet us at the library."

Sebastian stares at me, and I let my talent roam his mind. *Are you sure we should hide our talents? She did help us, after all.*

*It's just temporary. People act strangely when they find out that we're talented, and I don't want to share that yet.*

*That's true.* He stares at his hands.

"Are you two all right?" Maeve looks at us oddly.

I blink rapidly. She caught us talking between our minds. Of course we seem strange now. Just what I'd hoped to avoid.

"Have you lived here long?" I ask, changing the subject instead of answering her question.

Maeve's eyes widen. "This ramshackle place? Goodness, no. I was passing through, and this seemed like as good a place as any to stop for the night."

Sebastian frowns. "No one lives here?"

"Not as far as I can tell." She shrugs. "There is an extra room with two little beds. I'm guessing you could use a place to spend the night. I'd be happy to share this shack with you."

My heart speeds up. Maeve seems so nice. And it would be such a relief to let an adult take the lead again, even just for a little while. Staying focused through fear is exhausting. I feel Sebastian's thoughts mirror my own.

"Yes, please," I say.

"Thank you," Sebastian adds. Drat. Sometimes I don't quite remember my manners right.

"Of course," Maeve says. She pats my shoulder with a wistful expression, her finger catching for a moment on one of my long, tangled white locks. While she maintains a calm exterior, there's an undercurrent of sadness in every move she makes. It makes me want to reach out and hug her, though that would be too bold, even for me.

"Where are you headed?" Sebastian asks.

Maeve considers as she pulls out some food for herself. "I hardly even know. You see, my family is missing too."

Sebastian gasps. "That's terrible."

Her forehead creases. "I had a husband and three children, a boy and two girls. But I don't know where they are."

I frown. "But when did you lose them?"

"Years ago. I've been searching for them ever since.

Traveling through the three territories, hoping for some sign of them."

I finish my chicken and wipe my mouth with my sleeve. "What happened?"

Sebastian gives me a short look. *That's a little rude to ask…*

But Maeve doesn't think worse of me for it. If anything, her thoughts of us grow fonder by the minute.

"I don't really know. One day they were there, and the next, I was alone."

"Do you know who stole them?" I'm exhausted, and my mouth is asking questions before my brain can think better of it. I'm lucky Maeve is patient.

She sets down the last bite of her bread. She stares at it for a long moment, then shakes herself out of the funk.

"Yes and no." She sighs. "I tracked down the person who took them. But no one knows where they ended up after they left the culprit's hands. They could be anywhere."

Maeve finishes eating and stands. The moon rose outside the windows while we talked, and she lights a couple of candles, giving one to us.

"I don't know about you, but I'm exhausted from the day's

journey. I'm going to bed. The room for you two is just down the hall."

We wish her good night, then gather our meager belongings and head to the small chamber at the back of the shack. There are two cots set out, and the blankets are only a little dusty. A quick shake remedies that.

When I rest my head on the pillow, the full extent of my exhaustion begins to set in like a lead weight on my chest.

*These are much better accommodations than what we had last night*, Sebastian thinks. I startle; I didn't even realize my talent was loose.

But I smile at him across the space between our cots. *Much better indeed.*

He yawns and rolls over, worries about his sister and the looming body walker circling through his mind. I leave his thoughts to him and let my talent wander elsewhere. The night is still, though wild animals roam the forest. Bats hunting insects fly overhead, while a pack of wolves chases a deer who is nearly as tired as me and Sebastian. I yank my talent away from them and linger on the other creatures instead. Owls, raccoons, and opossums skitter among the trees, their trundling thoughts creating a warm background noise that I can't help finding soothing.

I drift off to sleep, lulled by visions of delicious insects and little ones whining to be fed.

In the morning, I'm woken by Sebastian's startled thoughts.

*Where am I?* Quickly followed by memories of the night before and meeting Maeve.

I sit straight up on my cot. "Thanks a lot," I say, then laugh.

Sebastian rubs his eyes sheepishly. "Sorry. It's hard to sleep. And waking up somewhere other than home or…" His voice trails off.

"I know. It's still confusing for me too sometimes."

He nods but says no more, and I keep my magic out of his head. I already know what he's feeling. I feel the same way.

We dress quickly and quietly, then make our way into the main part of the little house. Maeve is at the stove, cooking what smells like the most delicious scrambled eggs in the world. My belly rumbles. Who knew being on the run could leave one so hungry all the time?

Maeve brightens when she sees us. "Come, sit. I thought I'd make breakfast. It's much nicer to eat with friends." She pauses. "We are friends, aren't we? I don't mean to presume."

My face flushes at the unexpected declaration. I don't know that I've ever had a real friend besides Sebastian. Perhaps some of the other of the Lady's servants could be considered my friends, like Kalia the dream eater or Melanthe the mind mover, but no one was ever as close to me as Sebastian.

"Yes, I…I think we are."

A smile dances over Sebastian's face. "Friends it is," he agrees.

"Oh good. Here you are." Maeve puts a plate heaped with scrambled eggs and toasted bread in front of each of us.

The food is as delicious as it smells, and we waste no time digging in.

Maeve watches us while we eat, with an expression that sends my gut aflutter. The emotion behind it is something I know I felt long ago, but the memory itself is impossible to grasp.

"You still intend to go to the Parillan Archives?" Maeve asks.

I nod between bites. Sebastian kicks the leg of the table and sighs. "Yes, but it's not going to be easy," he says.

Maeve raises an eyebrow. "And why is that?"

"We know it's in Parilla, somewhere near the center. But that's about it. My sister was the one who knew the way."

I put my fork down. I had almost forgotten that unpleasant detail. It seemed like such a good idea until that whole bit.

"That will make things more difficult," Maeve agrees.

"And we aren't entirely sure where we are now either," Sebastian adds, glummer than before.

I scrunch my face. "Do *you* know where we are?"

Maeve laughs. "Yes, I do. I think I can help you with both problems, actually, and you can help me too."

My eyes widen. "How?"

"I know where we are, for one, and two, I happen to be carrying a map, so I can help you find the Parillan Archives."

"That would be amazing!" Sebastian cries.

"But how can we help you?" I ask.

Maeve's smile falters. "The truth is, I'm lonely. It's been rather depressing searching for my family alone. But the three of us, we have a common goal. There's something powerful in that. And the Archives might hold the key to finding my family too."

For a moment I am unable to believe our good luck. But then I let my talent dip into Maeve's thoughts. They're warm and hopeful, over the same familiar undercurrent of loss.

There's no trace of a con or lie.

I give Sebastian a quick nod, and he grins.

"We'd love to travel with you," I say. Relief floods over me. We're safe. We have someone to protect us, someone to guide us on our journey.

We're no longer alone.

# CHAPTER EIGHT

Early the next morning, we leave the little shack behind along with the mystery of its missing owner. Maeve has decided we'll stop by the first village we find to get enough supplies to feed all three of us. When I blurted out that we had no money for food, she laughed and told me that she was not without means and was happy to provide for us as long as we traveled together.

Maeve is kind and generous. She walks tall and proud like Lady Aisling did, but with none of her wickedness. None of her conceit.

For a time, I attempt to mimic her stride as we walk through the woods. The way she carries her head, her arms. But my legs are too short, and I can't quite get my arms to swing in the same manner. Sebastian gives me a puzzled glance.

*What are you doing?*

I grin. *I like the way Maeve walks. Like she's strong and fearless. I want to walk like that too.*

He nods, understanding. When you've spent years living in constant fear, surrounded by those who feel the same, it isn't easy to walk tall, even after your fear is in the past. Maeve is undaunted. Calm and kind. Strong without cruelty. She's everything Lady Aisling was not.

Her mind is more disciplined than most people's too. Though I try hard to keep my talent in check, every once in a while I accidentally dip into her thoughts. But they remain the same: sadness and determination. And with a touch of lightness now that we're all traveling together.

As we walk, Maeve tells us stories of her journey.

"Did you know that there are trees in Abbacho as big as a small mountain? I found an entire grove while I searched there for my children. People reside in them too. One even has a house carved out of the living wood, way high up in the branches." Her face is animated, and her auburn hair shimmers while she speaks.

I laugh. "That sounds impossible. I can't even picture it."

But Sebastian sobers next to me. *I've been there once*, he thinks. I quickly stop laughing. I know precisely what he was doing there. He doesn't have the luxury of forgetting like the rest of us did.

"Well, it is quite a sight to see. If you ever find yourself in Abbacho, I highly recommend seeking it out."

Sebastian stares at his shoes. *I miss Jemma. She should be here with us.*

My thoughts worm into his mind. *Don't worry. Your sister will meet us at the library. Then everything can go back to normal.*

He flashes me a half smile, and I leave his thoughts in peace.

"How do you think they grew so big?" I ask Maeve.

"I have no idea. I didn't think to stop and ask them," she says with a wink, making me laugh.

"What else have you seen?"

"Many things, child. So many things." For a moment, a serious expression flits over Maeve's face, but it's quickly replaced with a smile. "One of my other favorites was a jungle, deep in the reaches of Abbacho. All sorts of strange flora and fauna abound there. It was one of the most beautiful places I've ever been."

Sebastian frowns. "Isn't the jungle supposed to be dangerous?"

"Oh, very. Snakes as thick as tree trunks, wildcats that can blend in so well you'd never see them until you were their supper. Even the plants might try to eat you. But sometimes the most dangerous things are also the most beautiful."

Maeve is right. Lady Aisling was once the most beautiful woman I'd ever met, but undoubtedly the most dangerous. I shudder. I wish I could ban all thought of the Lady from my head and just live as though she'd never stolen my life from me. Sometimes I've thought about asking Sebastian to remove all memories of my time in Zinnia, not just the really bad ones.

But if I didn't have those memories, I really would have nothing at all. Even though the scattered memories I have of my time under the Lady's thumb are unpleasant, they're still better than nothing.

Soon the trees begin to thin out, and signs of civilization appear. It isn't long before we find ourselves on a cobbled road and can just make out the rooftops of a village in the distance.

My stomach rumbles. While Maeve has kept us fed, I'm looking forward to not having to ration what she has left among the three of us. Sebastian is thinking the same thing.

"Almost there," Maeve says, a heady sort of anticipation trilling over her that I can't help but feel too. I pull my talent back. I don't want to be rude.

The closer we get to the village, the louder all the minds become. My hold on my magic is as tight as possible; otherwise, I could become overwhelmed quickly.

The village is small and quaint, and people smile at us as we make our way to the center where the shops are likely to be. The constant hum of thoughts buzzes around my head, but I breathe deeply and let it flow past me as best I can. Somewhere, someone is playing music on a stringed instrument, the notes dancing with those from a flute. I keep my thoughts focused on that as my feet skip along of their own accord after Maeve.

"Hold on, little one," Maeve says, a firm hand on my shoulder. She stops at a shop entrance—a grocer's—and I nearly dance right by. But she just smiles. "There will be plenty of time for dancing later, I promise."

Maeve isn't put off my outbursts of strangeness, which is a relief. We enter the grocer's shop, and she quickly purchases some food. She even lets us each pick out a sweet from the cabinet on the counter.

"Where are you folks headed?" asks the grocer, a short old man wearing a blue apron.

"The Parillan Archives," Maeve says. "It's in the mountains just over the plains beyond your village, isn't it?"

The grocer nods, then narrows his eyes at us. "It is. Though good luck getting in there. They're serious folks and rather picky about who they let within their walls."

"Oh, I'm sure we can convince them. We're researching her family line." She places her hands on my shoulders. "And I'm certain they will find it to be an intriguing mission."

The grocer hands Maeve her change and shrugs. "Well, best of luck to you then." He watches us as we leave, and I can't help but glance back and take a quick peek at his thoughts.

*Poor folks. I hope they don't have their hearts too set on the library. I can't imagine them succeeding...*

I nearly trip over the step leaving the shop. He seems certain, but then again so does Maeve. She holds her hand out to me and helps me stay upright. I squeeze her fingers in thanks, and we move on.

I trust Maeve. She knows what she's doing. And I'm sure she won't lead us astray.

# CHAPTER NINE

I awake the next morning determined. I've decided that I must be honest with Maeve: I have to tell her the truth about who I am and why I'm seeking the Parillan Archives. She'll find out sooner or later. Once we get there and I have to explain exactly what information I'm searching for, I won't be able to hide why. The longer I hold off, the more insulted she'll probably be.

I don't want her to be hurt. And I especially don't want her to leave us.

I just hope she doesn't feel the same distaste for the talented that too many others do. Sebastian knows my plan but remains undecided if he will share his role just yet. I can tell my secret just fine without revealing his.

The morning sun spills over the mountains in the distance, alighting on our small camp on the grassy plains. Maeve yawns from her bedroll and stretches. My heart lurches into my stomach.

I must do this now before I lose my nerve.

My feet carry me to her side before I can think better of it. When I kneel next to her, Maeve tilts her head.

"Good morning, little one. You look so serious today."

My mouth opens, but nothing comes out. Maeve sits up straighter, concern clear on her face.

"What's the matter, Simone?"

I shake my head and try to speak again, this time with more success. "Nothing's wrong. I need to tell you something." My throat has grown rougher than burlap, but I clear it the best I can.

Maeve sits all the way up and faces me. "Go on."

My hands twist together, and I stare at them while words pour from my mouth. "I haven't been completely honest with you about why I'm going to the library."

"All right," she says, her face unreadable. My talent

remains under a tight grip. I don't think I should let myself read her mind yet.

"Have you heard of Lady Aisling and her Garden of Souls?"

Surprise flits over Maeve's face. "I have."

I turn my eyes back to my twisting hands. "I was one of her captives. Which means I have a talent. Mind reading. The people who rescued us tried to find my family, but it was no use. There was a memory stealer under her control, too, so I don't even know what they looked like. All I have is a location to help me find out what happened to them, but no one has ever heard of the village. We thought a record of it might be somewhere in the library."

My mouth snaps shut, and my limbs feel strange and loose all of a sudden. I can't bring myself to face Maeve.

But I don't have to.

"You poor thing," Maeve says, then wraps an arm around my shoulders. "Thank you for trusting me enough to tell me. I hope the Parillan Archives can help us both."

My heart begins to settle into a normal pace again as I lean into her embrace. "You're not angry?"

She laughs. "Not at all. You were right not to tell me at first. That's a fearsome talent, and one that some might want to take advantage of. You have to be careful and protect yourself." She squeezes me a little tighter. "But now that you know me a little better, I'm glad you decided to confide in me."

Relief warms me. I shall have to tell Sebastian when he returns from gathering berries for breakfast. Maybe he'll want to confide in her too. But I'll leave that choice up to him.

"Do you know when Lady Aisling took you?" Maeve asks.

I frown. "No. Long enough ago that all trace of my village— Wren—seems to have disappeared. I even asked the Lady myself a couple days ago, but she couldn't remember."

Maeve raises her eyebrows. "You faced your captor yourself? You're brave." I blush. "And if Lady Aisling can't remember when she took you, that must mean you are very old. She must have had a life bringer talent in her garden—and a youth keeper, too, I assume?"

"Yes, which has made this all more confusing, really."

"Don't worry, if there are answers to be had in the Archives, we'll find them." She squeezes my shoulder. "I'm glad you told me."

"I was afraid you wouldn't want to be around me. Most people think me strange."

"I have never minded strange," Maeve says, releasing me and standing up. "Now, let's fix ourselves some breakfast."

I stand too, feeling lighter than I have in a very, very long time.

I have no idea how far we've traveled or how long we've walked, but it feels like forever to me. It's a good thing I have Sebastian and Maeve here to keep me on the path. It seems like at every turn there are new, inviting ones that could lead to somewhere intriguing. I would be hopelessly lost on my own, so distracted by every trail I could take that I'd never be able to keep to the one I need the most.

But with them by my side, I have only gotten sidetracked here and there. Long enough to run my hands over a strange new flower or leaf, or to greet a small bird or animal nearby. Every now and then, I have to let out a burst of energy with a twirl or skip ahead, but they always anchor me. The comforting feel of their minds is the tether that prevents me from floating away on the afternoon breeze.

We left the deep forest this morning as the terrain became hilly, then mountainous. The library is supposed to be here somewhere on one of the highest peaks. We've let Maeve lead the way. I suppose we've been accustomed for so long to letting someone else lead that it's second nature to us. Falling back into the habit is a relief.

Both Sebastian and I feel a little safer having someone else in charge.

Safe enough that Sebastian even decided to tell Maeve about his talent. Of course, she embraced it as warmly as mine.

Maeve is happiest this way too. When we first met her, her thoughts were forlorn, but now that she has someone to look after, they're brighter and more hopeful.

Perhaps we found what we need in each other.

We started up the mountain near midday, and now our feet ache from all the marching. At least we're well fed, thanks to the supplies Maeve bought at the last village. The sun dips low in the sky, and the shadows encroach from the east. There are curious animals here and there, especially a mama fox and her cubs who have been trailing us ever since they saw us stop for a snack late in the afternoon. The mother's thoughts reveal how hungry she is and hopeful for an easy remedy for her and her babies. Without letting Sebastian or Maeve see, I quietly remove some of the beef jerky from my bag and sprinkle it behind me.

I smile, hearing the elated thoughts of the mother fox and the little squeals of her babies.

For a moment, Maeve frowns. "What was that?"

I smile innocently. "I didn't hear a thing."

Sebastian looks at me funny, and I shrug. Maeve turns back to the trail.

"It's getting late. Hopefully, we'll find the Archives before nightfall," she says. A hint of worry tinges her words, and I slip into her mind.

*And they'll let us stay with them*, she thinks.

I stumble over a root, but catch myself. Why wouldn't they let us stay? Maeve said she has means and money, and Sebastian and I are willing to earn our keep. I want to ask, but I don't want her to know I've been reading her mind without permission. I bite my curious tongue.

But now worry begins to color every step. The forest seems

a little darker and deeper, the animals a little louder. The clouds gathering overhead almost seem to form a frown in the sky.

Sebastian notices, of course. *What's the matter?* he thinks at me, but I just shake my head. He's feeling much less fearful since we found Maeve. There's no sense in both of us being scared. Hopefully, all will be well and we'll have no trouble.

Just when I fear I can move no farther and that we must've climbed two mountains at least, we reach a break in the trees and catch a glimpse of what lies ahead. I suck my breath in between my teeth sharply enough that it whistles.

Before us is a tall peak, capped by an enormous circular stone building. It is the largest building I've ever seen, even from this distance—next to Lady Aisling's mansion, of course. But this is more imposing. The gray stone is lit up by the setting sun, giving it a dusky purple hue. It's more of a fortress than what I'd thought a library would be. It must be to protect all that knowledge inside.

Sebastian's thoughts are as awed as my own.

"Well," Maeve says, also clearly impressed. "I suppose that must be it." She grins back at us, her gray eyes sparkling. "Not quite what I expected, but hopefully it holds the answers we all need."

Her hope is infectious, rolling off her in waves, and it buoys me up too.

"Do you think we'll get there before nightfall?" Sebastian asks.

"If we hurry. Are you two feeling up to it, or should we stop to rest?" She considers us. I straighten my spine.

"I'm ready," I say, and Sebastian nods his agreement.

"Then let's get going."

We strike out once more, the giant structure now always in sight, getting a little closer with every step. The incline becomes steeper, but our steps don't flag. There are only a handful of animals this high up, mostly birds. Their thoughts are sleepy and filled with settling into their nests. I wish *we* were settling into a bed, but I know we still have a little way left to go.

When we finally reach the doorstep of the library, my head buzzes with exhaustion. Sebastian is nearly asleep on his feet. The only thing keeping me awake is the ache all over my body. I'm vaguely aware of Maeve knocking on the heavy wooden door and the keen-eyed woman who answers. I can't focus on the words they exchange, but she seems to need some convincing. Eventually the door opens, and we trip inside. The woman's expression appears confused, but I chalk it up to my exhaustion. I'm careful to keep my magic close. I need their help; I don't wish to start off on the wrong foot by invading their privacy on their threshold.

Through lidded eyes, I see hints of stone walls and candles lining the way through a long corridor. Just when I believe I couldn't possibly take another step, a door opens and we're shuffled inside a room with several cots. Someone—Maeve, I think—sets me down on the nearest one. It feels like the softest bed I've ever slept in. Her shadow looms over me, and soft lips whisper over my forehead. *Sleep well, little one*, she thinks.

And I do.

# CHAPTER TEN

When the sun wakes me the next morning, I ache everywhere. I groan and roll over to find I'm alone. The room is small but contains three cots. I suppose this must be where they keep unexpected guests.

Reaching out with my talent to search for any familiar minds nearby, I can sense Sebastian dreaming in a room next to me and Maeve awake in the hall. I leave my bed behind to join her. Her face lights up when she sees me.

"Simone. How did you sleep?"

I stretch and yawn. "All right. But I'm sore. I'm not used to walking this much anymore." When I traveled with Lord Tate and Alden, they usually gave me a pony to ride or brought me on the horse with them. I love to wander, but in the last couple of days, I've seen more than I ever have in my life. Well, that I can remember, anyway.

"Have you talked to the head librarian yet?"

Maeve sighed. "I'm waiting for her now."

"Do you think they'll let us stay?" I swallow hard. At the moment, my greatest fear isn't the body walker; it's that we'll never find the help we need.

Maeve brushes a wayward lock of my wispy hair from my face. "Of course they will. How could they possibly say no to you?"

My throat constricts. We haven't shared with Maeve that the librarians visited us once before and did exactly that. But this time, under different circumstances, and with very little effort required on their part, I hope they'll agree. Jemma thought they would.

Sebastian's door cracks open and he peeks out, rubbing his bleary eyes. "Morning," he says. His dark curls are even more mussed up than my pale locks, and that makes me giggle.

The sharp *clickety-clack* of shoes on stone rings out down the hall. A librarian I recognize—Rachel, the book binder—turns the corner with an odd look on her face. She startles when she sees me and Sebastian.

"Oh!" she says. "It's you two. I didn't realize that. Ida and I just arrived last night too." She gives Maeve a sideways glance. "Where is your sister?" she asks Sebastian.

He turns a distinct shade of green and scuffs his toe on the floor. I speak instead.

"We got separated from Jemma. She's supposed to meet us here soon." Another lie, another bit of truth. I wish to be wholly honest with these people, but at the same time I worry they might send us away if they believe we are connected to a body walker. It's a delicate balance and not one I'm juggling well at all.

Rachel frowns. "I see. Well, I'm afraid she isn't here. But hopefully she'll arrive soon."

I nod vigorously, and Maeve raises her eyebrows. I glance at my feet.

"We happened upon one another while traveling," Maeve says. "And decided it would be best to travel together since we had the same destination in mind."

"Our head librarian, Euna, will meet with you now to discuss what you hope to accomplish here." Rachel gives me another long stare, then leads us down the hall. "I'll take you to her."

The corridor is lined with windows, and I can't help peeking outside as we pass. We're only on the first level of the fortress, but we're high enough that we can see nearly all of Parilla—and probably parts of Zinnia and Abbacho—from this height. The world looks both enormous and tiny at the same time. The view is dizzying. Maeve taps my shoulder, and I realize I've stopped to stare.

"Come, child. There will be time for that later."

I glance at Rachel and am relieved to see that she's smiling. We continue, and I do my best not to let my eyes stray back to the magnificent sight beyond the windows. Like Maeve said, there will be time later.

But before we reach our destination, we turn a corner and see someone else I recognize—and wish I hadn't. Ida raises her eyebrows at us and then sticks her nose in the air as she walks by in the other direction. Of course, she would be here. Rachel, however, doesn't seem concerned at all, judging by the smirk that plays on her lips.

It isn't long before Rachel brings us into a cozy sitting room with a warm fire and several overstuffed chairs set around it. I stretch my hands toward the flames instinctively. I love how they dance. But then the head librarian enters the room, and I immediately feel her irritation as she takes a seat. I'm not even trying to use my talent, so her temper must be quite short this morning. That doesn't bode well for us.

I tuck my hands into hidden pockets in my skirts and give the woman my attention.

"Welcome to our library," Euna says. She is a tall woman, with long, gray hair braided down her back and sharp hazel eyes. "To what do we owe your unexpected presence?"

Maeve speaks first. "We seek knowledge and understand that this is the best place in the three territories to acquire it."

Euna raises an eyebrow. "And what knowledge exactly are you seeking?"

"The whereabouts of our families. My children have gone missing. And this girl, Simone"—Maeve puts her hands on my shoulders—"is searching for her family too."

Rachel steps forward. "Simone was one of Lady Aisling's captives, ma'am. She has a talent."

Euna seems surprised. "Really? And what can you do, my dear?" She leans toward me.

"I'm a mind reader," I say. "But I try not to do it without permission."

"Of course," Euna says thoughtfully.

"All I know of my family is that they lived in the village of Wren somewhere in Parilla, possibly long ago. But no one has ever heard of Wren. We were hoping there might be some record of it in your archives."

"Ah, then you don't know *when* the Lady took you," Euna says. The irritation she exuded when she first entered has dulled and is turning toward warmth. Maybe even sympathy. Or perhaps that's just the fire. I'm too nervous to peek into her mind to find out for certain. I doubt she'd appreciate that, and it wouldn't be the best way to start if we want to be allowed to stay here.

"We don't have any researchers to spare at the moment," Euna warns. "You would have to hunt through our collections yourselves. It will be tedious and may take a long time. And even then, we can't promise results. But if Wren really did exist and any maps or scrolls about it survive, they will be here."

Hope rises in my chest and flies out my mouth before I can stop it. "Does this mean we can stay?"

Rachel laughs, and Euna speaks. "Yes. Rachel will take you

to the wing with available rooms and show you where the books you need might be. And she will show you where you can get some breakfast too. I have no doubt it was a long journey, and you must be famished."

She stands and takes her leave, though not without a sideways glance at Maeve, who seems relieved.

I'm relieved too. After our experience with Ida, the older librarian, I was afraid Euna would say no. But now that that's settled, my stomach growls so loudly, I can't hear over it. Breakfast first, then everything else can come later.

Rachel brings us to a larger room that perhaps was once filled to the brim with people from the three territories visiting and learning, but that number has slowed to a trickle. Or maybe we're just late for breakfast. I never was good with time.

A large round table set out with breakfast stables sits in the center of the room. Bowls of fruit, hard-boiled eggs, sausages, breads and cheeses, muffins, and griddle cakes—my favorite—make my mouth water.

"This is where we meet for breakfast, lunch, and dinner. We have excellent cooks on staff," Rachel says. "Please help yourselves. I'll return in half an hour to bring you to your quarters, and then I'll show you where to begin your research." She ducks back through the doorway, leaving us with the food and a handful of other librarians and researchers.

Sebastian wastes no time digging in, piling his plate high with muffins and sausages. I follow suit, helping myself to some griddle cakes and fruit. Maeve does the same.

"They're my favorites," she says, and I flush. It's almost as if she could read *my* mind.

We find a table and begin to eat. Sebastian's mind is aflutter. *How long do you think it will be until Jemma gets here too?*

*I don't know. I guess it depends on how long the body walker takes to release her.* I immediately regret my thoughts as Sebastian nearly chokes on his muffin. *I'm sure she's on her way by now. Maybe just a couple days more.*

*I hope so*, he thinks.

A few minutes later, a woman joins us. She's about the same age as Jemma, with light hair and eyes so dark brown they almost seem black. She has a huge grin on her face that's more startling than anything.

"Welcome to the Parillan Archives! I'm Devynne. I hear you two"—she gestures to me and Sebastian—"are talented." She beams. "I'm studying the origins of the Cerelia Comet and magic itself. I'd love to pick your brains."

The way she looks at us gives me shivers. Sebastian nudges me under the table.

*I don't like how she said that*, he thinks.

*Me neither.*

"Perhaps another day," Maeve says gently. "We've only just arrived and have much to do."

Devynne waves that off. "Of course, of course. But please, before you leave, I must sit you both down and learn about you and your talents." She leans back in the chair and sighs. "Isn't it wonderful how many talented there are around, now that Lady Aisling is no more? Who knew she had trapped so many of those poor people in that garden of hers, all just to hoard their magic for herself?"

I shudder. The urge to run tugs at my legs. Sebastian's eyes are wide and panicked.

"Let them eat their meal in peace, Devynne," says a man's voice. A stern-looking fellow in dull-gray robes stands behind us. "Some of us have serious research to do and don't need to have you prattling about talents and comets all the time."

Devynne laughs. "This is Connor. He thinks anyone who takes joy in their work is a fraud." She leans forward. "I wouldn't be as staid as him for the world. But, I will leave you to your breakfast. And hope to run into you in the stacks." She whisks away, giving Connor a dirty look as she passes. I can't help but take a quick, little peek...

*Pompous idiot*, Devynne thinks.

*Charlatan*, Connor thinks.

I laugh, then clap my hands over my mouth. Connor frowns, his bushy eyebrows making a deep V on his forehead.

"What is so funny?" he says.

"N-nothing," I squeak out.

He grunts.

"And what is it you're researching?" Maeve asks, no doubt trying to lighten the mood.

Connor straightens up and clasps his hands in front of him. "I'm from Zinnia, and I'm researching the lost city that once thrived in a valley near the current capital. I've examined the ruins extensively, and now I'm hunting through the archives for any references others may have missed. I am quite thorough."

"I see," Maeve says. "Good luck to you."

He nods curtly and leaves the dining hall in a hurry.

*Children in the library? It shall not be borne.*

The angry force of his thoughts nearly shoves me off my chair. I shakily put down my fork, all hunger vanished.

"Well, he didn't like us much," I murmur. Maeve puts her hand over mine.

"No matter. We have permission to be here, and we will do what we came here to do. I can promise you that."

# CHAPTER ELEVEN

By the time we finish our breakfast, Rachel returns and leads us down another corridor to the living quarters. She shows each of us to our own small room containing a bed, a chair, and a little table with a candle and washbowl. Each one has a window that looks out onto the mountain below.

"I had your bags brought here for you. Here are your keys. Now, would you like to see the archives?" Rachel grins. She must really love it here. Everything about the way she moves, speaks, even thinks, proves it.

"Yes, thank you," Maeve says.

A spring is in Rachel's step as she leads us deeper into the fortress and up to the second level. She tells us about the paintings on the walls—who made them, and when. All the names and dates jumble in my head until I worry they might fall out my ears. I don't know how she manages to keep all that straight. But I'm rather impressed that she can. When we reach the landing on the second level, she takes us directly to a set of large double doors and opens them wide.

Sebastian gasps, while I'm stunned into silence. Maeve seems unfazed, as though this is exactly what she expected. The room is a gigantic circle, lined with tall shelves and row after row after row of books and scrolls. The room encompasses the entire level of the building, vast enough that I can't even see all the shelves from where I stand. The shelves are all made from the same dark-brown wood, but the books themselves vary in color and size, more so than I'd imagined. Here and there, glass cases dot the space, along with paintings and tapestries hung on the walls. Many librarians are on this level, sitting like statues at the workstations that line the windows, or darting about the stacks on the hunt for just the right book. Despite the silence, the electric hum of activity is in the air.

"I had no idea this many books even existed!" I say.

Rachel laughs. "And there are five more levels just like it."

*How will we ever find what we need?* Sebastian thinks at me.

*Maybe Rachel or Maeve will have some ideas to narrow the search.*

*I sure hope so…*

"The oldest books on this level are in the northwest section over there," Rachel continues, pointing to shelves. "There are reading tables scattered throughout. If you need help, let me know." She leans forward conspiratorially. "I'm only an assistant for now, which means that unlike the other librarians, I have a little more free time."

*And I disagree with the mandate that we only work on paying projects*, Rachel thinks. I do my best to hide my smile.

"That's kind of you, Rachel," Maeve says. We head toward the section of the library that she indicated and begin to scan the bindings of books for ones that might include old villages of Parilla. Maeve pulls down a few and sets them on a table, pushing one toward me and another toward Sebastian.

"This is as good a place to start as any," she says. Together we begin to peruse the books, searching for the keyword that could alter my life if we find it.

*Wren.*

We spend what feels like hours poring over books and scrolls, but to no avail. It doesn't help that I keep getting distracted and wandering to see what interesting treasures are elsewhere in the stacks. Sebastian does his best to be studious, but he can't help worrying about Jemma, so his progress is slow. Maeve helps us hunt for Wren for a time, then heads to the section containing more recent town records, hoping to find any hint of newcomers matching the description of her three stolen children. Every city, town, and village in the three territories sends their records here for storage. I can tell from brushing over Maeve's thoughts that she doesn't really expect to find them, but hope is a strange thing.

Several times during our search, I can't help feeling as though someone is watching me, but when I glance over my shoulder, no one is there. I'm doing my best to be good and not eavesdrop on anyone accidentally, but after the third time it happens, there's no help for it. I reach out with my magic and land on thoughts that give me chills.

*Intriguing children. I don't know how they tricked Euna into letting them research here, but they might prove most useful after all…*

I startle, recognizing that mind. Ida, the librarian who

visited us with Rachel in Sebastian's village. Curious, I get up from my seat until I can actually see her, just around the corner from us. She's moving around the library reshelving books. When she notices me staring at her, her expressions turns to a frown.

"If you're not going to work, you may as well go home," she snaps, then returns to her task with her back to me.

Her sharp retort is cutting, and I share it with Sebastian when I return to our desk.

*Well, that's just unkind,* he thinks. *I didn't like her before, and I still don't.*

*Me neither.*

By the time we decide to stop for the day, we're exhausted and my nose itches with dust from the books. As we head out the library doors, we walk right into Euna and Connor—and they aren't happy.

"You can't be serious!" Connor says.

"What's going on?" asks Maeve.

"Everything is fine. Don't worry yourselves," Euna says. Connor huffs and straightens his jacket.

"Everything is *not* fine. These children are underfoot in

the library. This one"—he points at me, causing my face to turn beet red—"isn't even studious. She spends more time humming and driving me up a wall than researching whatever she's here for!"

I hadn't even realized Connor was on the same level of the Archives as us. Sometimes I don't notice all the things I ought to when I wander. I stare at my feet, but Maeve puts a comforting hand on my shoulder.

"She's a girl searching for her lost family, not a researcher like you. She certainly didn't intend to bother you. If it happens again, let us know, and we'll move to a different level of the library."

"See? There's plenty of room for you both here," Euna says.

Connor grunts. "We're not finished," he says to Euna as he stomps off down the corridor. I let my talent skim across his mind.

*Unreasonable, foolish woman. If she won't do something about them, I will...*

His words make me shiver, but I keep it to myself.

Euna sighs and smooths her skirts. "My apologies, Connor is passionate about his work and sometimes gets rather frustrated when things don't go as he'd like. Are you headed to dinner now?"

"Oh yes," Sebastian says, his stomach growling. "I never knew how hungry reading could make you."

Maeve and Euna laugh.

"Well, enjoy it. Good night." Then Euna enters the library herself, letting the double doors close behind her.

"Between him and Ida, it doesn't seem anyone likes having us here." Sebastian says. We head for the dining hall, even though my feet grow heavier with every step.

But once we sit down to eat, I begin to perk up. There are more people here for dinner than there were earlier in the day, and the clamor of thoughts is almost deafening. I have to struggle to hold back my magic, but lately I've been finding it a little easier. Perhaps all the practice is finally beginning to help.

As I take my last bite of potpie, the violent heat of angry thoughts sends me spinning in my seat so fast I nearly choke.

"Simone, what is it?" Maeve says.

Connor stands in the doorway of the dining hall, scowling at our little group. He growls and walks out without bothering to eat. I shiver and turn back around.

"He won't bother us," Maeve says. "I'll make sure of it."

I smile weakly at her, but that can't hide how uneasy Connor makes me feel. Something about him strikes me as vicious. And we're already on his bad side.

# CHAPTER TWELVE

We've been at the Archives for a whole week. Now, instead of wandering through a garden or stream-lined woods, I wind my way through a forest of books. Some ancient and crumbling, others crisp and new, there are plenty of places for me to explore, and not as many anxious minds as there were in Sebastian's village. In fact, I'm usually the noisiest thing here. Sometimes I laugh without thinking, disrupting the silence, and find myself shushed by the nearest librarian.

The library is set up in the round. The center of the building is a vast staircase that seems to curl up to the sky. The main floor houses living quarters for the librarians and guest rooms for people like us, as well as the kitchen and dining areas. I don't even know how many floors there are, but all of them are filled with books and trinkets. The whole place aches with the weight of history. On each level, the shelves are tall and towering, made from a dark wood grain that is smooth under my palms in the newer areas and rough and worn in the oldest parts.

We've examined what Rachel suggested might be useful in the first two tiers of the library, and now we're just waiting for access to some of the oldest manuscripts that are housed in a separate section on another floor. I imagine it will be dark and quiet as a tomb there, with only thin candles for light. And the ink on the scrolls has faded to a nearly unreadable weight.

But really, I don't know. Not yet. Maeve is working on getting us access. She has been a great help and seems almost as eager to find my family as I am.

Today, Sebastian and I wait at our usual reading table on the second floor, while Maeve is at her own table on the other side of this floor. She keeps a log of notes and a stack of books and papers she's using to try to piece together what happened to her missing family. Every second she isn't helping us, she spends there.

"Are you ready?" Rachel's voice startles me out of my thoughts.

"Oh yes," I say, hopping off my chair. "I'll go fetch Maeve."

Before Sebastian or Rachel can say a word, I'm off, skipping through the long rows of shelves toward where Maeve sits. I slow as I approach her desk. It isn't nice to startle people, and I'm trying to be more mindful of bursting headlong from the stacks.

Maeve has her back to me as I approach, but she glances behind and smiles. She tucks the thin, little book she was examining back into the stack on her table.

"Simone! Is Rachel already back?"

"She is. I've come to fetch you."

"Then we should hurry." Maeve holds out her hand. I gladly take it and return the grin. When we regroup, Rachel leads us up to the room housing the old scrolls and maps, and whistles as she thumbs through the keys on the key ring at her waist. "I've only been in here once before. We don't usually grant new visitors access. The head librarian has clearly taken a shine to you." She finds the key she needs—an old iron one, the handle twisted into intricate knotwork—and unlocks the heavy wooden door. She holds it open, and Maeve leads us inside.

In the center of the room is a heavy oak table that looks as though it was hewn from the cross section of an ancient, enormous tree. Maeve told us about trees like that in Abbacho, but I don't recall if I've ever seen them. If I did, Sebastian must have taken the memory away from me. I run my hands over the table and shiver.

The rest of the circular room is shelf after shelf packed with scrolls of all shapes and sizes, with pockets of manuscripts stacked flat and a few bound books here and there with crackling leather covers. Something scents the air—a smell particular to books, as I've discovered over the past few days—and makes my nose itch pleasantly. My mouth hangs open as I take it all in, while Sebastian sputters beside me.

"How will we ever find what we need in here without it all crumbling to dust?" he says, turning in a circle.

Rachel laughs. "That's what you have me for." She puts a finger to her chin and twirls. Impulsively I mirror her, my skirts and hair spinning wildly for a brief moment. Rachel runs a hand over the faded alphanumeric system imprinted on each shelf until she finds what she wants.

"Aha!" She pulls down a sheaf of papers that look like

maps, along with a few old scrolls, and sets them down on the huge oak table. "Here we are. These are our oldest maps and show the very beginnings of town records in the three territories. The rest of the records are on those shelves to your right."

I take in all the piles and piles of records, momentarily succumbing to hopelessness. "But where do we start?"

Rachel pats me on the shoulder, brushing back my frizzy white hair. "Don't worry. I'll stay and help. Your little group is by far the most interesting search I've been given since I got here."

*They think they're tasking me with something tedious, but how wrong they are!* she thinks, and I laugh.

Rachel's eyes widen, and then she laughs too. "Sorry, I forgot for a moment there that you can read minds."

I shake my head sheepishly. "No, *I'm* sorry. I didn't mean to let my talent roam freely." I scratch my head. "It's been hard to keep it under control since Lady Aisling lost her powers. I'm not certain, but I believe I had better control once. But only vague memories to prove it."

Sebastian frowns and looks away.

*Sorry*, I think at him. *It isn't your fault. It's hers. Only hers.*

He gives me a small smile, but it's half-hearted at best.

"Let's get started, shall we?" Rachel says. She begins assigning each of us a stack of records and maps to sort through.

Sebastian's eyes widen, but he says nothing. His mind, though, is daunted. *This is going to take forever,* he thinks.

I shrug. *All I have is time.*

His mind strays to thoughts of his sister as he pores over the stack set before him, and I immediately regret my words.

*I wish Jemma was here. I really thought she'd be here by now,* Sebastian thinks. *What could have happened to her? We shouldn't have left her.*

*I'm sure she'll be here soon. And there wasn't anything we could have done for her. The body walker would've just gotten us, too, if we'd stayed.*

We both shudder, knowing all too well what that would mean.

I begin with the maps Rachel set beside me. They're old and crinkle around the edges, little bits crumbling in my hands as I unroll them. One of the few things I recall from my time with Lady Aisling is how to read a map. Lord Tate showed me, though he despaired at getting me to remember. But some of it remained in my mind. I was just too distracted, too filled with spells at the time for much else other than commands.

But I know how to read the compass on the map and which markings are for streams and rivers, trees, and villages. The first is of Parilla, detailing an area I've passed through before. I believe it was while the Lady's lieutenants had us chasing Emmeline, the shadow weaver, as she fled her home. The village of Wren is not noted on it, even though the map is quite old.

I pull another map closer and try to focus, but my mind begins to wander, and soon my feet follow. I circle the room, fingers trailing over the worn spines. There is so much information in this one room, let alone the entire building, that I can't help feeling like a mind could burst before taking it all in.

Something stops me, and I realize Maeve's hands are on my shoulders.

"Little one, I know it is hard, but we need to focus on the task at hand. Do you think you can try for a little while longer?" Her face is kind and her mind clear of anger, but my cheeks redden anyway.

"Sorry," I say, staring at my feet. My shoes are still dirty from the hike up the mountains last week. It's the only pair I brought with me. "I'll try harder."

Maeve squeezes my shoulder. "That's all. I know it's

difficult for you after what the Lady did. But I have faith you can do it with a bit more practice."

Hope rises within me. Wouldn't it be lovely if I find my family, she finds hers, and Jemma arrives soon too? That's all I want. All of our families to be reunited. Everyone back where they belong.

I return to my spot at the huge round table and begin my search with renewed gusto. I will do this. I will try my hardest. For me, for Sebastian. And for Maeve.

The afternoon passes in a blur. It must be nearing dinnertime when I finally spy something. Excitement jolts through me. I hesitate, my hand hovering over the edge of the map beneath my fingers. I was about to put it in the pile with all the other maps that didn't pan out, but now I'm glad I didn't. In the upper corner, nearly faded, are four letters that make my heart skip.

*W-R-E-N.*

"Rachel!" I cry, trying to keep my hands from shaking.

The librarian raises her eyebrows and stops at my side. Her eyes widen. "Well done, Simone. I think you found it."

Sebastian gasps. "Really? You found Wren?" He hurries over to me, and so does Maeve.

My heart thrums so fast I fear it will fly right out of my chest. I don't dare close my eyes, terrified the map will disappear if I do. That map contains the only remaining link to my family. It's a fragile thread that could just as easily vanish. Maeve smiles down at me, and I give her a shaky grin. I've been searching for my family for so long that it doesn't seem possible this could be real.

Rachel turns to another section of the room. "Let's see… That's a *very* old one. I don't recognize some of these surrounding landmarks. We'll need to compare it to a more recent one to determine where it really is now."

I hold my breath while she fumbles through a couple other stacks of maps. Maeve whispers in my ear. "Good work." I beam, my heart racing faster than ever. Dizziness threatens as Rachel finally pulls another map depicting the entire Parillan territory over to the table and spreads it flat for us all to see. She compares the two maps, her frown growing deeper by the second.

The warmth that was rising in me begins to cool. "What's wrong?" I ask, peering around her arm.

"I..." Rachel hesitates, glancing back and forth between the ancient map and the newer one several times. "I don't understand. It doesn't make any sense."

"What doesn't?" Maeve asks, taking the older map from Rachel. She sighs when she sees what Rachel did.

Dread claws its way up my back. "What's wrong?" I ask again, more insistently this time.

Maeve gives me a long, sad look. "My dear. I'm sorry. I don't think we're going to be able to visit Wren after all."

She places the small older map just above a portion of the newer one. She points to the location noted. "Wren is here, in a valley between these two mountain ranges." She moves her finger to the newer map. "But the mountains are no longer separated by a valley—Lake Uccello lies between them. At some point, the area must have flooded, removing any remaining trace of the village."

Disappointment cuts through me. I sink to the floor, head in my hands. Sebastian sits down next to me with a hand over mine.

*I'm sorry*, he thinks. I don't respond. I don't know how. I suspected I must be much older than I appear and that I was taken long ago, but I never imagined it would be so long that the entire landscape of my former home would be underwater. I'd hoped it would be more like Sebastian's situation where he still had family, but they'd just grown up now.

My breath grows ragged and I *hurt*, everywhere and nowhere all at once. This is how it feels to have every ounce of hope wrung from my heart.

Someone lifts me up and curls me against their chest. Auburn hair falls over my face, and Maeve's voice whispers softly to me. "I know it feels like daggers now, but the pain will lessen with time."

Maeve understands. She lost her children, her hope of finding them faint and her grief huge. Though it has lessened since we found her. I nestle into her shoulder, unshed tears stinging the corners of my eyes, and she carries me back to my quarters.

She sets me gently in my bed and pulls a blanket up to my chin, humming a lullaby. I close my eyes, letting her soft, comforting voice lull me into a fitful slumber.

# CHAPTER THIRTEEN

When I wake, it's late evening, but Maeve is still asleep in the chair near my bed. I don't wish to wake her, so I quietly creep from the room. It feels as though a leaden weight drags on my every step. I hope Maeve is right about it lessening over time.

But there is something I must do.

I knock on Sebastian's door, and it opens moments later. He breathes out, relief clear on his face. "I was worried about you," he says, holding the door open wide.

I enter his room and spin to face him, letting my skirts tickle my ankles as they settle back down.

"Are you all right?" he asks. "I can't imagine what you must be feeling after what you discovered."

I sink into the chair in the corner of his room, letting the cushion swallow me up. "Sort of," I say, wrinkling my nose. "I guess I never really thought we'd find it. So it's not a surprise, but for one moment there, I so hoped—almost believed—there was something left to find. It hurts to have that hope dashed." I rub the center of my chest.

"I'm sorry," Sebastian says. And what else is there to say? I know if he could, he'd give me back my memories of my family. But he can't, so I have truly lost them for good.

"Thanks," I say. I give him a half-hearted smile. "I'm glad you at least found your family."

I mean it kindly, but it makes Sebastian frown, setting his mind to worry about Jemma's tardiness.

"Don't worry," I say. "I know Jemma will be here soon. I'm sure of it. She'd never leave you." I lean across the space between us and squeeze his hand. "We're family too. And you'll always have me. It may sound strange, but however horrible Lady Aisling was to steal us, it did bring us together. You're basically the only family I have."

Sebastian squeezes my hand fiercely. "And you have a place in my family. Always, I promise."

"Thank you," I say, taking a deep breath. "But there's something we need to do."

Sebastian gives me a quizzical look.

"We need to talk to the head librarian, Euna. I want to thank her. It's important to me that she knows we found what we needed and that we'll be leaving as soon as Jemma joins us."

I head for Sebastian's door, but he stops me. "You want to go right now?"

I shrug. "I'd rather do it sooner than later. And we can stop in the kitchens on the way back to have some dinner. I'm starving, and the dining hall must be closed at this late hour."

Sebastian comes with me through the dark halls, and we walk in a comfortable silence, my eyes roaming farther than my feet. Every hallway here is a little different, yet also much the same at the rest. The same dark, wood-paneled walls and gleaming stone floor, polished to a shine by countless feet over the centuries. But Sebastian's hall has glass cases of strange things dotting the corridor. Small statuaries of important figures from long ago, ornately painted bowls with swooping curves, and other fascinating little objects that claim my attention. As we near the library level, huge tapestries line the walls, each one a story just waiting to be discovered. I can't help but stop at every one. Sebastian practically has to drag me away.

We know Euna is a night owl, so we decide to check her office first. It's a small room on the third level, walled off by glass from the rest of the library, where she keeps special artifacts and manuscripts and her current research. But she isn't there when we arrive, and no candle burns inside. The room doesn't look like it's been used for hours.

Instead, we hurry to the head librarian's living quarters. We knock on Euna's heavy door, but no one answers.

*Do you think she's sleeping?* Sebastian thinks.

*Doubtful. I haven't seen her retire early once since we've been here.*

*Maybe her research took her to a different part of the stacks than usual tonight?*

I consider. *Maybe. Let's try once more first.*

We knock again, louder this time. Two minutes pass and still no answer.

I've done my best to keep my talent to myself while we've

been here. I know most people don't appreciate it when someone else glimpses their innermost thoughts. But a sudden fear grabs me, and I must know. Something seems odd about the situation.

I let my talent loose, sending it under the door and searching the room for Euna's thoughts or dreams if she's asleep.

Instead, I find nothing at all.

My talent searches the other sleeping quarters nearby; again no Euna, only her fellow librarians.

I grab Sebastian's shoulder, my fingers digging into his skin. "She isn't here. Something isn't right."

Sebastian tries to stay positive. "Maybe she went to the kitchens for a snack? We were headed there anyway after here. Might as well check."

I breathe deeply. "Yes, you're right. There's probably a perfectly reasonable explanation."

But uneasiness coils in my gut, twisting my innards into disarray. The awful feeling tiptoes behind us, all the way down the stairs to the lower levels of the great building where the kitchen sits. Sebastian opens the door, the warm smells of roasted chicken and freshly baked bread enveloping us.

The cook waves when we enter. "I was wondering if you

two would come by." This isn't the first night we have ventured down here late like this, though usually it's also with Maeve. The cook pushes a couple of plates toward us and gestures to the chairs by the fire. "Come, eat. Too many researchers get faint from spending all day in the stacks and forgetting to eat a crumb."

We gladly do as she says. The food is delicious, but I barely taste it. All I can think about is the head librarian.

"Have you seen Euna this evening?" I ask the cook while she finishes cleaning up.

"Not since dinner, no. She retired to her chambers, I imagine."

My leg bounces up and down, sending stray bits of chicken from my plate into the fire.

*I don't like this*, I think to Sebastian.

He manages to keep his composure. *Me neither.*

*We have to find her.*

We finish our food and quickly head out. Too often, it's difficult for me to focus on a single thought for long, yet fear seems to be the one thing that keeps my focus sharp and all-consuming. My breath is ragged as we snake through the halls of the library fortress. Sebastian grabs my hand and squeezes. That makes me feel a little better, and I know it comforts him too.

We look out for each other. We protected each other from the Lady as much as we could then, and we always will. We won't be victims ever again.

As we make our way through the halls, I begin to wish that I'd woken Maeve after all. She could've helped us, and if she wakes and I'm gone, she might be worried. But we're almost up to the top tier of the library, so we may as well finish what we've begun.

Our legs begin to tire and our clasped hands have become sweaty, but we don't let go. Panic boils over inside my chest, and I let my talent roam freely, desperate to locate any sign of her. While I don't find Euna, this time I find someone else. Ida is awake, and I can sense her curious, calculating mind on the same tier as us. Her thoughts make me think she may be at our worktable, shuffling through the books we left behind this afternoon.

*They claim they're looking for Wren, but maybe there's something more here about Lady Aisling...*

Ida's interest in Lady Aisling—evident from the first time

we met—is unsettling at best. She's much too eager to investigate her particular research topic for my liking. It makes how she regards us all the more troubling.

I swallow hard and hurry Sebastian up to the next floor. Euna must be here somewhere. She can't have just disappeared; that's impossible without a spot hopper, and as far as I know, there isn't one anywhere near the Archives. The only talented person here besides us is Rachel, and her book binding magic can't account for disappearances. So far we've only encountered a couple of librarians burning the midnight candles, like Ida, and many, many dreaming minds.

Until we reach the second-to-last floor of the fortress. An angry mind makes me halt in my tracks, and Sebastian stumbles into me.

*Foolish good-for-nothings. They never understand the importance of my research.*

Connor. The researcher from Zinnia. I yank my talent back.

*What is it?* Sebastian thinks.

*Connor. He's nearby, and he's not happy.*

*You don't think he'd do anything to Euna, do you?* Moonlight slips in through the slanted windows of the stairwell, making Sebastian's eyes shine.

I bite my lip. *I hope not. He seems harmless enough, just grumpy.*

Neither Sebastian nor I like Connor, and the feeling is mutual. He's been nothing but rude to us since we arrived.

*Let's keep out of sight,* I think. We duck into the nearest room. The shadowed silhouettes of row after row of books on shelves greet us as we wait for Connor to storm by.

He sweeps past our door, angrily muttering to himself about his own importance and that of his work.

When he's gone, we tiptoe back into the hall and continue our upward trek, my talent grazing over the rooms we pass for any hint of Euna. Finally, we reach the last level. We scour the entire loop, every room, even every closet. Dread wells up inside me, making me dizzy. I send my magic out in as wide a net as I can, hoping against hope that I pick up something, anything, that feels like Euna.

Nothing, nothing, nothing.

*Hold on,* Sebastian thinks, tugging my hand to lead me toward the far side of the fortress. There's still one place left that we haven't searched. He gestures to a narrow flight of stairs that leads up to the roof, partially hidden by the stacks of books. We waste no time, but halfway up, I pause.

For one brief instant, I felt Euna's mind. Her thoughts were jumbled and confused. Then gone again.

I swallow hard as we open the hatch to the roof and step out into the cold night air. I pull my skirts closer as if that could make them lend me more warmth. Sebastian rubs his arms.

There—on the other side of the railing surrounding the roof—is a figure in a dressing gown, her skin and hair glowing against the dark backdrop of the night.

"Euna!" I cry, reaching out with my talent at the same time. I half expect her to turn around with a smile and ask us what we're doing up on the roof with her.

She doesn't turn. And when I touch her mind, it doesn't have the familiar contours of the steady, thoughtful woman we've grown used to.

She isn't there. But someone else is.

Then they're gone, vanished before I can grab hold of that foreign mind. Euna's thoughts become a violent storm as she teeters near the railing. We break into a run, grabbing at her clothes to pull her away from the edge. Finally she turns, her eyes wild and confused, seeing us but without full recognition.

"Where am I?" she whispers. Then she crumples to the stone roof.

*Where did I go? Where did I go? Where did I go?* rushes through her brain in a painful loop. I pull my talent back and wrap my arms around my waist. My whole body quakes, and I can't tell if it's from the cold or the fear rattling my bones.

Sebastian crouches near Euna. Her eyes have begun to roll back in her head, and I worry she may lose consciousness. "We have to get her help. Can you tell what happened to her?" When he glances up at me, his face is as white as a sheet.

I brace myself on the railing of the roof as he reaches my side. "What is it, Simone?"

I shake my head, my pale curls wisping across my vision. "They're here. They got her. I don't know what they wanted, but they left just as I called out her name."

Sebastian takes a step back. "No. That's not possible. We left the body walker behind. We're supposed to be safe here."

"If it's a body walker we're dealing with, we're not safe

*anywhere.* We'll never be safe, our friends will never be safe, *no one* will ever be safe. Not until the body walker is stopped for good."

# CHAPTER FOURTEEN

We prop Euna up near the door to the stairs, safely away from the edge of the roof. She is too tall for us to carry down ourselves, and we're too terrified of the body walker to split up.

We hurry down the stairs, shouting for someone, anyone to come and help. When we reach the next level down, we are met with a librarian rubbing her eyes. She probably dozed off in the stacks.

"My goodness, what is the matter?" she says.

"Euna is on the roof!" Sebastian cries.

"She was attacked by a body walker, and she needs help. Please, hurry," I say.

The woman wastes no time. "Find the doctor. Her name is Olga. Her quarters are on the third floor. Her suite is the fourth door on the right from the stairs. I'll see to Euna until she arrives."

Sebastian and I hurry away, and when we reach the third floor, we count the doors until we reach the fourth one, then knock as if our lives depend upon it. We're scared that Euna's does.

We know how it feels to be used by a body walker. Hollowed out, exhausted. Like something inside you is off-kilter, and you have no idea how to set it right again.

A bleary-eyed woman answers the door, wrapping a robe around her wiry frame. "What is it, dears?" she asks. "Is someone hurt?"

"Yes. Euna needs help. She's on the roof."

Her eyes widen, all trace of sleepiness slipping away. "Let me grab my bag."

Other librarians begin to open their doors to see what's going on. Even Devynne and her insatiable curiosity peek out into the hall. But Olga takes me and Sebastian firmly by the elbows. "Take me to her, and tell me what happened."

"We were looking for her earlier this evening. We wanted to thank her for her hospitality," I say.

"But we couldn't find her," Sebastian adds.

"We searched everywhere and didn't find a trace of her until we reached the roof," I say.

Olga frowns. "Did she tell you what she was doing all the way up there?"

I shake my head. "She couldn't. A body walker had taken her over. I don't know why they would have brought her all the way up there, but—"

Olga stops and faces me. "Hold on. A body walker? That's a rare talent and quite an accusation. What makes you so certain?"

I wrap my arms around my middle, and Sebastian instinctively places a hand on my back. "I'm Simone, a mind reader. Both of us"—I gesture to Sebastian—"were in Lady Aisling's garden. She used the body walker's talent on us. I'd recognize it anywhere. But mostly because I could see Euna's body, but not hear her thoughts. Not until the body walker let her go."

"That's when she collapsed," Sebastian says.

Olga briskly picks up the pace again. "Then I suppose you would know," she muses. "I have never treated someone who has had their mind used in such a manner. It's a good thing we have a team of researchers here who might be able to help if she doesn't recover quickly."

Hope nearly lifts me off my feet. If the researchers here decide to investigate body walkers, perhaps we can help too. Or at least be privy to the fruits of their research so we can protect ourselves and those we love, like Jemma, in the future. Sebastian's thoughts have been straying to his sister every few minutes since I told him the body walker had been controlling Euna. I wonder where Jemma ended up when the body walker left her. I know Lady Aisling was able to control more than one of us at a time, but that was by using her special potion made from the body walker's flowers. I expect a real body walker can do the same thing. I truly hope Jemma is free of the body walker's grasp by now and somewhere safe.

When we reach the roof, we find the first librarian we woke up hovering over a very confused Euna. Her eyes can't quite seem to focus on anything. Instead, they flit like a hummingbird from one object to the next. Olga kneels next to her and begins to do a cursory examination.

"Well, she doesn't seem to have a head wound, and there's no physical damage I can see." She leans back on her heels. "But whatever happened clearly affected her mind. It may indeed be a body walker, just as you say."

"A body walker?" Maeve's voice yanks my attention away from Euna. She stands in the doorway to the roof. She must have heard the commotion and followed us up here.

"Yes, it's a plausible explanation for Euna's sudden strange condition. Come," Olga says to the other librarian. "Let's get her down to her quarters where she'll be more comfortable." Using a portable stretcher contraption from Olga's bag, the pair of them manage to get Euna down the stairs and take her away. Maeve, however, remains behind with us.

"What happened here?" she asks. "When I woke and you were gone, Simone, I was worried. Then I heard people shouting about something happening on the roof. You two scared me half to death." She brushes her hair back and places a hand on her chest. Real concern leaks from her thoughts, enveloping me.

But all I can do is stare at my shoes. We've kept this from her. The fact that we were fleeing a body walker. It's strange—and frightening!—that they would show up here too. Unless, of course, we somehow managed to lead them here. The very thought steals my breath.

Sebastian stares at me wild-eyed as the full brunt of that fear falls over us both.

But why would they follow us? That is the part that defies explanation. The Lady is powerless now, so we know it can't be her, but perhaps it is happening again. Maybe someone is hunting talented folks. We've had too many encounters with the body walker for it to be a coincidence.

"There was a body walker here. They took Euna over, then left when we found her," I say.

Maeve's face pales. "Are you sure?"

I nod vigorously. "Lady Aisling used that talent on us all the time. We know how it works intimately. Her mind was shoved down. Someone else was in there controlling her."

But Maeve seems unconvinced. "That's certainly a terrible thought. But maybe there's another explanation. How could a body walker just sneak in here? This place is a fortress."

Her words strike a terrible chord. What if they were already here? We know many librarians travel for research, like Ida and Rachel did. It could be any of them who just took a less winding path to get here. Except Rachel, of course, since we already know she's a book binder, and Euna since she's the latest victim. It could even be one of the researchers. I wouldn't put it past someone like Connor, or even Devynne.

Without knowing for sure, there's only a handful of people here we can really trust.

"Besides, with Lady Aisling's powers gone, there's nothing to fear," Maeve continues.

We exchange a glance.

Sebastian finds his voice first. "We haven't been entirely honest with you about that." He glares at his feet. "My sister was taken by a body walker too. That's how we became separated."

I can't look at Maeve. My cheeks flame, and rocks churn in my belly. "When I finally caught a glimpse of her mind, she told us to run and that she'd meet us here."

Maeve's gentle touch cools the heat of my embarrassment.

"I understand," she says. "That must have been terrible for you. All alone with no idea who you could trust." She puts her arms around us both and draws us in. We melt into her. "I hope you can trust me now."

"Yes," Sebastian and I both murmur. And we mean it with all our hearts.

"Then trust this: I will keep you safe. The body walker

will not harm you. Not while you're with me. I promise you that."

My shock at her certainty lets my talent slip for a moment and peek at her thoughts. Her mind is as orderly as always, and her certainty about this is unshakable. I remember Jemma's promise to protect us and how it was undercut by her own fears over who would protect her. There's nothing like that in Maeve's mind.

"How can you be sure?" Sebastian asks. "I thought we were safe with my sister, and I was wrong about that."

Maeve holds us at arm's length, a serious look on her face. "Because I will fight for you with everything I have. I'm sure your sister loves you, Sebastian, but is she a fighter?"

He shakes his head. Jemma was kind and thoughtful, but definitely not a fighter, that's for sure. But Maeve is. I can tell. From the way she holds herself to her ordered mind, I can tell she doesn't give up, and she's stronger than anyone I've met who isn't talented.

"Well, there's your answer. I'm a fighter. And I'll protect you at any cost. Now, let's get you both inside."

We let Maeve lead us back to our quarters, feeling a strange mix of fear, hope, and gratitude.

# CHAPTER FIFTEEN

The day after the body walker attacked Euna, the library was in disarray. Researchers gossiped, and librarians were tasked with searching the stacks for more information about warding off body walkers. But by nightfall, Euna had regained her wits, though not her memories of that time, and the fearful urgency occupying the residents of the library lost its edge. Within a week, the attack seemed all but forgotten by everyone but me and Sebastian.

But we continue to search for ways to deal with body walkers while we wait for Jemma and Maeve does her own research for her family. Seeing our concern, Rachel continues to help as well. And she still keeps an eye out for any other references to Wren for me. It's likely any town records were lost when it flooded long ago, but we're still hoping to find out more about how long ago the valley flooded and what happened to the families that once lived there. If they moved somewhere else, perhaps I can still find them. But mostly, I explore, wandering through the stacks like a wayward leaf caught on the wind.

I keep my distance from most of the librarians and researchers. The realization that any of them might be the body walker has me skittish around them. Especially Connor, who is still as grumpy as ever, and Devynne and Ida too. Ida's attention leaves me cold. Somehow, she seems to be around nearly every corner I turn. Devynne's a bit too keen on learning about our talents. She's been hounding us for an interview, but Maeve rebuffs her every time. A thing we're grateful for. We don't wish to relive our time with the Lady any more than we need to. Our lives in the Garden feel further away with every tick of the clock.

Our days pass in a simple rhythm. One we begin to grow accustomed to. Every day, the fear of the body walker returning lessens. Maybe they ran into Euna and established their connection to her when she wasn't even in the Archives and just overtook her on a whim. Or perhaps they were looking for something and left. However strange it is that we had several near-misses with them, they don't seem to have been following us after all. Wherever they went, we're safe now. Though I still steer clear of Ida, Devynne, and Connor just to be safe.

Sebastian still worries about his sister, but Maeve has grown to be such a fixture in our lives that the sting has finally begun to fade. Some days he hardly thinks of Jemma at all. And when he does, he feels guilty for not missing her more. I've tried telling him not to feel guilty, that she'll no doubt join us soon, but it doesn't seem to help.

One morning, two weeks after Euna was attacked, I skip down the stairs ahead of Sebastian, eager for breakfast. Maeve isn't seated at our usual table when we arrive. She must've headed off to the stacks already. We eat a bowl of oatmeal and hurry to the third floor of the library. That's where we left off the day before, and I recall Maeve had found something that interested her there. I hadn't meant to peek into her mind, but I could feel her eagerness to investigate more.

But when we reach her favorite spot—a desk on the north side that looks out over the mountain range and a lush waterfall on the other side of the mountain—she isn't there. The books she was using the night before sit silently as if waiting for her to return and open them again. I run a hand over the words written on the spine of one: *A History of Rare Talents*. I frown. It sounds more like something Devynne would have on her desk than Maeve.

"Why do you think she was looking at talents?" I say aloud. Sebastian shrugs.

"Maybe she was researching body walkers too. Just in case." He shivers involuntarily.

I brush the same chill off my shoulders. "Well, we can ask her when we find her. I guess she must still be sleeping."

Sebastian's frown is mirrored by my own. Maeve isn't normally one to sleep late. Usually, she rises before both of us. But maybe she's meeting with a librarian or even Euna herself about whatever she found yesterday.

I brighten at the thought. "She must be meeting someone first."

Sebastian looks a little relieved. "Yes, that does make sense."

The weight off our shoulders, we return to our little table nearby and the books we'd been examining the night before.

Today is particularly difficult because all I can think about is when Maeve will appear. The hours tick by, and still no sign of her.

By lunchtime, I've begun to worry. No one we've asked has seen Maeve today either. Knocks on her door don't draw her from her room, and the lock doesn't want to budge. Maeve has made it clear that she doesn't want me to use my talent to eavesdrop on her thoughts, so I resist checking, even though an unpleasant feeling gnaws on the tips of my toes. Where could she be?

I know—I *know*—she wouldn't abandon us. I've been inside her head accidentally before. I've seen how much she cares for us.

Finally, I can't stand it any longer. My nails have been gnawed to the quick. I push myself off my chair, startling Sebastian.

"We have to do something. I can't just sit here."

"Maybe we can ask Rachel for help." Sebastian points to the book binder who just walked through our level of the library.

I practically leap in her direction. "Rachel!" I yell, and she turns around to see me barreling toward her. Her first response is to laugh, but her face falters when she sees my expression.

"Simone, what is it? What's wrong?"

"It's Maeve. I'm worried. We haven't seen her all day, and she isn't answering when we knock at her door. No one else has seen her either."

Rachel considers for a moment. "You know, I don't think I've seen her since last night. Quite late too. She said she was going out for a walk."

I frown. "A walk? But when?" When I saw her last, she was headed to bed.

"Oh, well after midnight. She was doing some late research and needed to clear her head."

I grab Rachel's arm, fear racing through every limb. "Something's happened. Can you help us find her?"

"Of course. But don't worry, I'm sure she's fine." She brushes my hair back from my face and ushers Sebastian and me into the hall. "She's probably still sleeping, but it wouldn't hurt to check." Despite Rachel's words, there's an undercurrent of something in her thoughts that makes me uneasy.

*How odd... No one's seen Maeve, just like Ida... There must be a reasonable explanation...*

I stop short and stare at Rachel. "What do you mean, just like Ida?"

"Simone! You shouldn't do that," she admonishes me, and I lower my eyes to the floor. She's right. I should have been paying better attention. Rachel sighs. "But now that you know, yes, no one has seen Ida today either. Which isn't like her at all. I was actually looking for her in the library when you found me."

Sebastian gasps. "That can't be a coincidence."

Rachel puts an arm around each of our shoulders. "Don't worry. Let's just check Maeve's room and see if she's there."

When we reach the door to Maeve's quarters, my heart is in my throat, all sorts of terrible scenarios racing through my head. But out of respect for Maeve's wishes, I keep my magic pulled back. For now. Rachel finds the master key on her key ring and unlocks the door, my heart skipping as the tumblers turn. She opens it gently, and I push past her into the room. Light streams in through the windows, illuminating Maeve's folded clothes on a shelf and rumpled sheets on the bed.

Maeve herself is nowhere to be found.

It's as if she vanished into thin air. Her bag is missing too.

My hands begin to shake, and I shove them into my pockets, but Sebastian stops me. He takes one and grips it tightly in his own.

We're both thinking the same thing: the body walker has come for Maeve.

# CHAPTER SIXTEEN

**M**aeve is gone. I can hardly breathe. We need her. She swore she'd protect us, but the body walker stole her away. I just know it. The body walker may have taken Ida, too, for all we know. As much as I appreciate my own talent, there are times when I despise magic, especially those who would use it selfishly and with no regard for the consequences for others. What could the body walker possibly want with Maeve?

*What if they're trying to get to us through her? For our talents?* Sebastian thinks. *Why else would they keep appearing so close to us?*

My spine goes rigid. He's right; our protectors keep disappearing. *That's more possible than I'd like.*

"Simone?" Rachel says, looking back and forth between us as if she's been speaking and we've been ignoring her. Which is probably exactly what happened.

"Sorry," I manage to sputter out.

Rachel puts a hand on each of our shoulders. "Don't worry, I'm sure there's a simple explanation. We'll keep looking for both Maeve and Ida. I'll let Euna know, and I'm sure she'll send out a search party."

"Maeve isn't lost in the woods," Sebastian says.

Rachel frowns. "What do you mean? She went for a walk. It was late and dark, and if she was tired, it would be easy for her to get disoriented…"

"It was the body walker." I spit out the words like some foul-tasting thing. "They must have gotten Ida too."

Rachel looks like she's been slapped, but then her face changes to consideration. "I hope you're wrong, but you're right that we can't rule out that possibility. Not yet anyway. It is certainly very odd that they've both disappeared at the same time. Let's find Euna. She'll know what to do."

She leads us to Euna's chambers, but Sebastian and I never let go of each other's hands. That thin connection is our lifeline, the only thing keeping us both from flying off into endless panic. We find Euna in her sitting room, poring over an ancient tome. She looks up when we enter and puts her spectacles down.

"What is wrong?" she asks.

"Maeve is missing!" I cry. Rachel places a firm hand on my shoulder.

"No one has seen Ida today either. Her disappearance is a mystery, but we have two theories about Maeve," Rachel says. "She may have gotten lost in the woods when she went for a walk late last night, or—"

"Or the body walker has returned and taken her!" I can't contain myself. Panic has become a physical thing crawling out of my throat and over my skin.

Euna swallows hard. "Send out a search party immediately." Rachel ducks away to do as Euna instructed. We move to follow her, desperate to do something to help find Maeve, but Euna stops us. "Now, please sit, both of you. Tell me why you think it might be the body walker."

We confess everything to Euna—from our fear of the body walking talent as used by Lady Aisling to my first glimpse of it in use by the real owner of the talent in Sebastian's village to Jemma's predicament. When we finish, she folds her hands in her lap. Her face has grown sallow and bears a green tinge now.

"That's how you knew a body walker had taken control of me."

"I could feel their mind shoving yours down," I say. "It was as if you weren't even there."

Her hands quiver, though she tries to conceal it from us. "Bits and pieces of that night have begun to come back to me. It was the strangest feeling. Like I was a puppet and someone else was pulling the strings. I thought I was sleepwalking at first, but my body didn't respond. It wouldn't stop. And I swear I could hear a soft voice echoing inside my head. But mostly I was just confused. It was as though my eyes could only half allow me to see what I was doing. It was the most terrifying experience of my life. I wouldn't wish it on my worst enemy."

My back grows cold. "Then you understand why we must find Maeve. If the body walker has her..."

"It's unthinkable. And you feel responsible. For Ida, too, I'm sure." She gives us a watery smile. "That does you both credit. I know you care for Maeve, and she cares for you. But body walkers are dangerous. You must stay here, safe in our library, until they are found."

My jaw drops. "No! We must search for her too."

"We can't sit here and do nothing!" Sebastian moans.

Euna expression hardens. "You must. If the body walker is after your talents, we must protect you at all costs. No one wants to see the two of you captured again."

The meaning that slips between her nice words is that no one wants to see a body walker abusing powers like ours. Not after Lady Aisling.

I shudder. We don't want that either. But it's one thing to worry on my own; it's another to hear the same from an adult. That makes it seem all the more real.

But Euna won't hear it. She waves away our objections. "This is not up for debate. Absent your real guardian, Jemma— and now Maeve—you are my responsibility. Come, I will keep you safe."

As we discover, Euna's idea of keeping us safe is to lock us in one of the private suites and post a servant outside the door at all hours of the day. At least she imprisoned us together and ensured we had dinner brought to us. But I can hear the worried wonderings of the servant just outside. Our suspicions about the body walker are spreading through the fortress and making people nervous.

No one knows what body walkers really look like. This one could already be here, and we'd never know until it's too late.

But I've felt the shape of their mind. I know the tenor of their thoughts. I'm the only one who can find them.

Staying still is impossible. I pace the room, making a figure eight around the chairs set out by the fire.

*What's wrong?* Sebastian thinks. When we first arrived in our current prison, we both agreed it was best to keep our conversations in our heads since the guard could overhear.

*I need to be a part of that search party*, I think.

He burrows deeper into his chair. *Why? They already have lots of people looking.*

*But not* me. *I can find Maeve by her mind, or if she's still the body walker's prisoner, I can find her by the shape of their mind. No one else can do that.*

Sebastian frowns. *Simone, it's too dangerous. Euna's right about that.*

I whirl on him, my hair flaring out like an angry ghost. *You'd rather be a prisoner here? We've just traded one prison for another. I can't be cooped up like this.* Tears begin to burn in my eyes. *I have to be free to go where I please.*

My feet begin to twitch, and I have to move again.

*Simone, please.* Sebastian begs. *Don't do anything rash. Don't leave me.*

*Come with me.*

He shakes his head, eyes wide. *I can't face the body walker. I can't do it.*

The pit of my stomach grows cold. I don't know if I can go without Sebastian. We've become two peas in a pod. I depend on him to help me stay focused on things I ought to think about. And he depends on me to keep him calm. But I can't abandon Maeve either.

*What if we find a way to protect ourselves against the body walker first? Or how to stop them?*

Sebastian shrugs. *Maybe…*

I immediately spin around and begin to pound on the door. "We need to speak to Euna or Rachel. We have to continue researching in the library. It's very important."

At first, the guard doesn't respond. But I keep pounding and shouting. I don't relent until I hear the servant's thoughts shift from annoyance to frustration to assent just to get me to stop banging on the door.

"Fine, I'll go get her!" the servant grumbles. I let my fist drop to my side and sink to the floor. My hand aches from all the pounding, and I can feel the sore spot on the side that no doubt will become a bruise.

It feels like forever before Rachel arrives. I've stopped trying to keep my talent in check; I'm too desperate to get out of this room and do something. I hear her worried thoughts before we see her.

*The poor dears. This must be hard on them. I hope Maeve didn't just abandon them. They'll be devastated if she did.*

Her words are a strike across the face. I steady myself on the wall. Maeve would never abandon us. Why would Rachel think such an awful thing?

It's the first thing I ask her when she opens the door.

"What makes you think Maeve would abandon us? She loves us!" I cry. Sebastian looks stricken, since this is the first he's heard of it.

Rachel swallows hard. "Now, Simone, it isn't polite to listen to other people's private thoughts without their permission. I thought Maeve was working with you on that."

I clench my hands into fists, but my head hangs in shame.

She places a warm hand on my arm. "I know you're upset about Maeve being gone and not being able to be part of the search party. It's all right."

"But what do you mean?" Sebastian asks. "What would make you think such a thing?"

Rachel's expression softens. "It was a careless thought. I just... I don't know."

"Has there been any word from the search parties?" I ask more quietly.

She shakes her head. "Not yet, but hopefully soon." She places her hands on her hips. "Now, I hear you urgently needed to speak to me or Euna. What's going on?"

"We need to go the library. We were looking at a promising stack of books yesterday that could contain information that would help with the body walker."

Rachel raises an eyebrow as she considers. "Well, I suppose it wouldn't hurt. Especially since I know you want to help, and I can't let you run off and search by yourselves." She stretches out her hands to us. "All right, I'll take you. But you must stay close and promise me you won't try to run away."

"We promise," Sebastian and I say at the same time. But my fingers are crossed behind my back. As much as I hate to lie to Rachel, I have no intention of remaining here once we find what we need.

# CHAPTER SEVENTEEN

We waste no time returning to where we left off. We split the remaining books in the stack in half, but Rachel also takes some to search through.

The terror that's been holding me hostage all day keeps my focus razor sharp. I don't wander, even though the words swim in front of my eyes. My talent remains alert, brushing over every mind in the building, just in case the body walker or Maeve returns. I no longer care that I'm invading other people's privacy; I must find Maeve, and I will go to any length to help her.

I don't know how long we work. My world has transformed into words and pages and dust, a fragile construction that could blow away at any second. It feels like hours before Sebastian shout-thinks to get my attention.

*You're going to go after Maeve no matter what, aren't you?*

My face grows hot, and I glance away. *I have no choice.*

*I like Rachel. I really don't like lying to her.*

*I like her too. But we need Maeve. I can't lose her, Sebastian. I just couldn't take that.*

*I know.*

I try to return to my book, but a sudden thought grips me by the throat and threatens to strangle me where I stand. I've thought about it before, but I never shared it with Sebastian, because I didn't want him to worry. But now…now I'm certain it's true. Sebastian sees my discomfort and rubs my arm.

*What's wrong, Simone?*

*I can't help thinking the body walker must be right under our noses.*

Sebastian's hand flies off my skin as if it's been burned. *You mean you think it's someone we know? Someone who's been here all along?*

*How else could they have gotten to Euna and Maeve without resistance?* I shiver. *What if Connor is the body walker?*

Sebastian shudders. *What would make you think that?*

*It's the tenor of Connor's thoughts. Forceful and determined. A stubborn unwillingness to see any other viewpoint. They remind me of the body walker's.*

Sebastian's hands ball into fists. *It has to be him. He hasn't liked us or Maeve from the minute we got here.*

*Or it could be Devynne,* I muse. *She may seem innocent, but who knows what she might be hiding. I haven't snuck into her head enough to know for sure. And she's definitely been much too interested in us and our talents.*

*What can we do about it?*

I give him my best grimace as I eye Rachel's back at a table near ours. She's lost in her book. If we were to slip away for a bit, I doubt she'd even notice…

*We're going to prove it. Come on.*

I slip off my chair, and Sebastian follows suit. Both Devynne and Connor are somewhere around here. We tiptoe toward the alcove where Connor usually does his research. But he isn't there this time.

*Let's see if we can find him in the stacks,* I think to Sebastian, and he gives me a quick nod.

I let my talent roam this level of the library, brushing against mind after mind until I find who I'm searching for.

*He's on the next level up.*

With a quick check that Rachel is still thoroughly engrossed in her research, we head for the stairs and circle around until we're positioned right behind where Connor stands in a row of books.

To our surprise, he's not alone.

*What do you think he's doing with Devynne?* Sebastian asks.

*No clue. But let's find out.*

We huddle down behind the books, listening carefully to the two researchers' conversation.

"What do you mean you didn't take it? Someone had to."

Devynne laughs. "What would I want with your books? I don't care a whit about your silly village."

Connor's fists clench. "It is not a village; it is a lost city. And the book in question is a journal I only got by begging for special permission from Euna, and now it is missing. What did you do with it?"

"What makes you think I'd care about a journal? I've got more than enough research on my own plate to want to take any of yours." She folds her arms across her chest.

Connor begins to look a little squeamish. "Let's just say our interests may converge slightly in this particular journal."

Devynne rolls her eyes. "All right, I'll bite. How?"

"It's rumored to have been written by a soul summoner. The last one known to exist."

Devynne stands up straighter. "Well, that is mighty interesting. I wish I *had* been the one to take it. But I swear to you, I'm not."

Curious, I peek inside Devynne's thoughts. She's telling the truth. But Connor isn't convinced.

"Who else would be interested in the last remaining record of one of the most powerful talents out there?"

"I have no idea. Maybe Euna decided to put it away. Have you even checked with her?"

Connor's confidence falters. "Well, no…"

"Why don't you go do that before accusing me of stealing from you?" Devynne huffs and stomps away down the aisle. We stay low so that she doesn't glimpse us while we wait for Connor to leave too. His thoughts reveal that he is loath to admit to Euna that he lost this journal. But nothing at all about Maeve or Ida. Not in either of their heads.

And neither of their minds feels like the body walker's does, much to my dismay.

*I'm sorry, Sebastian. I can't tell for sure.*

*Maybe you only know how their mind feels when they're using their talent?*

I consider. *Yes, that's possible. And if they're not using it right now, it would be harder to tell.*

Dejected, we return to the reading table and pick up where we left off. But my mind won't sit still. Maeve wouldn't leave us willingly, of that I'm certain. Ida, I can't account for, but she doesn't seem like the type to just wander off either. When she visited Sebastian's village, she was all business, and once she determined we weren't going to be much help, she wasted no time leaving. Both of them missing at the same time is very strange…

Suddenly my limbs freeze and my mouth goes dry.

Ida visited Sebastian's village the very day I first encountered the body walker. And Rachel reported another incident of a body walker in a village they visited on the way. They would've been on the road—possibly the very same road we were on—the day Jemma was overtaken. And Ida was here in the library when Euna was taken by the body walker too.

Ida isn't missing.

Ida is the body walker. She's taken Maeve.

The certainty of it floods my veins with fire. My hand latches on to Sebastian's arm, and he yelps.

"What is it?" he whispers.

My mouth flaps open, but no words come out. I lick my dry lips and try again.

"Ida."

Sebastian's forehead makes a deep V. "What about her?"

"No, *Ida*. It's her. She's the body walker."

Confusion and fear grab hold of Sebastian. "What do you mean? How do you know?"

*It's safer to talk like this,* I think to Sebastian. *Think about it. She's been nearby during every encounter we've had with the body walker. Plus, she knows we're talented. Do you remember the way she looked at us the first time we met her?* I shudder. *And she wasn't very fond of Jemma either.*

*Oh no. You're right. Poor Jemma. What if she's done something terrible with her?* Sebastian's eyes are wide and watery. *What if she wants to use us?*

I squeeze his arm. *I won't let that happen. We'll protect each other. If she still has your sister, we'll find some way to protect her too.*

But the more I think about it, the more I'm sure he's right. While body walkers don't have to be near their victims, I'm willing to bet Ida took Maeve and Jemma to draw us out. She probably didn't dare take us here at the Archives, where Maeve is always watching over us. But if she got rid of Maeve… Well, that makes us easier targets.

I try to focus on our task, but all I can think about is how to save Maeve without getting captured by Ida in the process.

It feels as though hours pass before Sebastian taps me on the shoulder.

*Are you really going after her?*

*You know I have to.*

*What if it's a trap?* he thinks.

*I'm sure it's a trap. But if you come with me, we'll protect each other, just like we always have.*

He sighs. *I will, but only because I think I found something that could protect us.*

"What?!" I say out loud accidentally, then clap my hands over my mouth. One glance around reveals no one but Rachel heard us, and she just smiles and shakes her head, then returns to her book.

*Why didn't you say so earlier? What is it?*

Sebastian slides the book he's been reading over to me and points to a paragraph in the middle of the page:

*The great Zinnian king Rufaldo consulted with the high priestess of the Comet and devised a plan to thwart the walker set on taking over the kingdom. He decreed that the mountain range behind the city be mined for obsidian so that his army could be outfitted with obsidian blades, arrowheads, and jewelry to protect the royal family and courtiers. Obsidian, said to be able to shield one's mind, was the sole thing that would prevent the body walker from taking the king's army for himself...*

I suck my breath in sharply. *Obsidian... I've heard of the shiny, pitch-black stone*, I think. *But we don't have any obsidian.*

A small smile creeps over Sebastian's face. *But the library does.*

I frown. *Where?* I don't recall seeing the black stone, but then again, it would've been easy to miss.

*In one of the display cases in the old map room. There's an alcove with relics. I remember seeing some obsidian knives and arrowheads there. I think there was a necklace too.* His expression darkens. *We'll just borrow them and bring them back. And as long as we do it quickly, the librarians will never know.*

A laugh begs to escape from my throat, but instead I fling my arms around Sebastian in a hug.

*Perfect!* I think. *We'll escape tonight after everyone else has gone to bed.*

# CHAPTER EIGHTEEN

After our supervised research in the library, Rachel brings us back to our suite and has dinner sent up to us. Once again, a servant is posted outside our door.

But we know how to get around them.

We wait until it's late at night and most of the minds in the building are slumbering to put our plan in motion. We're both dressed, with our bags packed and ready to leave, as I creep closer to the door. I begin to scream. Then I drop to the floor, making a huge thud.

*What on earth was that?* the servant thinks. He hesitates to leave his post, but then I begin to moan.

It does the trick. The servant opens the door to see what

the commotion is about. But Sebastian grabs the servant's arm. It's a recent memory, so it only takes a few moments for Sebastian to find the one of Euna instructing him to watch us and of why he came into the room. At first the guard tries to pull his arm away, but Sebastian works quickly.

Sebastian releases him, and the servant blinks rapidly. "I… Sorry. So sorry to intrude." He ducks out the door and hurries down the hall, his mind a mess of confusion.

Now the door is unlocked, and the hall beyond is clear.

We keep close to the walls and tiptoe down the corridor toward the stairwell that leads up to the library and the map room we need. My talent stretches out, keeping track of who's asleep and who's not. We're particularly careful near the hallways where librarians and guests are still awake in their chambers. It's nerve-racking and exhilarating at the same time. The fear we could get caught at any second, mixed with the fact that we seem to be getting away with it.

At least until we hear someone else in the hallway. Fear lights up our insides, and Sebastian and I exchange a terrified glance as the sounds get closer.

*What do we do?* Sebastian thinks.

*Find somewhere to hide. Quickly!*

While we're not yet on the floor with the maps, we are near a door into this level of the library. We duck inside and hide behind one of the shelves. We hold our breath, hoping the person in the hall—Connor, judging by his thoughts—will pass right by.

But we're not so lucky. Connor opens the door to the same room and stomps inside. He carries a candle, holding it aloft while he examines the spines of books on a shelf not far from where we hide.

*Be ready,* I warn Sebastian. *We may have to move quickly if he gets too close.*

Sebastian's eyes are wide in the dim light. *What do you think he's searching for at this hour?* He wrinkles his nose.

I shrug, but my curiosity has been piqued. I let my magic rummage around Connor's brain, surprised at what I find.

*It must be here. I need it to complete my research. Perhaps those foolish children took it back to their rooms. I can't imagine what they might want with a book such as that, but if they did, there will be hell to pay.*

As soon as Connor begins to move in a different direction,

the pair of us sneak out of the room when his back is turned. I no longer suspect he might be the body walker, but I'm still not willing to take any chances. I have no doubt he'd use any excuse he could find to have us out from underfoot in the library. Soon we're running down the hall, then up the stairs to the next level, and then the next, until finally we reach the floor with the map room.

Being sneaky is exhausting. And we haven't even left the fortress yet.

The map room is usually kept locked, but Sebastian already took care of that problem. We snagged the master key from Rachel's key ring before she locked us in here, and then Sebastian made her forget before she could even object. The guilt Sebastian feels at deceiving her clings to him like a thick fog. But it was a necessary evil.

We unlock the door to the room holding all the ancient maps and artifacts and look around.

*Where is the obsidian you saw?* I ask, and Sebastian points to an alcove in a far corner. An array of artifacts crafted from the same pitch-black stone sits on a shelf behind a pane of glass. This time, the key doesn't work—it must be only for doors—and we're left with no choice. My heart sinks.

I don't wish to deface any property in the library. The librarians have been kind and sheltered us. But we need protection from the body walker. Perhaps we can work off the debt of replacing the glass once we come back.

*Ready?* I ask Sebastian. *Stand back.*

I lob a heavy book at the glass. Much to my dismay, it only cracks, but the noise sends a shudder through us both. After a few tense moments, we relax. No one has come rushing down the hall outside, so we should be safe for now. I pick up another book, the heaviest I can manage to lift, and this time the glass shatters into tiny pieces on the floor. Thankfully, the artifacts aren't affected, and Sebastian manages to grab a couple of them—two necklaces—without getting cut by the glass. He hands one to me, with a shiny, black orb I could get lost in if I stared at it too long, and puts the other, an arrowhead on an old chain, around his own neck.

We slip back into the hall, guiltily leaving the broken glass behind. A telltale reminder that we did what we could, but it wasn't quite enough.

Leaving the fortress is easier said than done. While most of the librarians are indeed still asleep, there are a few night owls wandering around here and there, and we have to duck inside empty rooms several times to remain out of sight. Reaching the exit is the most difficult part. We're sure there must be another exit somewhere in this beast of a building, but no one has ever told us where. Nor do any of the minds we narrowly miss have any knowledge I can glean from them about that.

Instead, we make our way to the main entrance of the building. There's a guard posted there who I spy by his thoughts. He's sleepy and wishing he hadn't agreed to work the second shift.

My magic ranges through the guard's mind. We use the same trick we did before: Sebastian approaches and makes him forget why he was there in the first place. As soon as he wanders off, confused, we waste no time running for the bulky wooden doors, then gingerly open them.

*Freedom*, I think, startling Sebastian.

*Don't run too far ahead*, he replies.

*Don't worry, I wouldn't leave you like that.*

We close the heavy door behind us as softly as possible. With any luck, the guard won't even notice anything is amiss and our flight won't be discovered until tomorrow morning when they don't find us in our beds. The cool night air slithers around our shoulders in a welcoming embrace, but it makes me shiver too.

Somewhere, hopefully not far away, is Maeve. We'll find a way to get past Ida and return with Maeve to nurse her back to health—whatever it is we must do to return her to normal. I may not know exactly how, and I may not know where we'll find her.

But I do know one thing for certain: we are not alone out here.

# CHAPTER NINETEEN

There's one great difference between Sebastian and me—I welcome the night, while he's terrified of the darkness. Or, more specifically, the things that lurk in the darkness. But I can sense them, feel their thoughts, and determine whether they are friend or foe. If we need to avoid something nearby, I'll know.

With the stars twinkling over our heads and the chill of night seeping into our bones, we forge ahead into the mountain woods hand in hand. I lead the way with my talent. Near the main path into the woods is an owl's nest, and an idea occurs to me.

*Just a moment*, I think to Sebastian, and he gives me a nervous glance. When he hears the hoot of the owl, he cringes.

An owl gave him that scar on his face, and they've terrified him ever since. But we don't need to get close to this one.

I let my talent brush over the mind of the owl in the tree. It's a mother just returning from the hunt. Her babies chirp and mew, happily eating the dinner she brought them. She feels safe and happy, and I take advantage of that by worming my way inside. Her mind is an open book, and I nudge in thoughts of Maeve and what she looks like. The owl's hackles raise, but she soon calms at my soothing thoughts. She shows me that Maeve passed by last night, at nearly the same time—just as she was feeding her chicks. Maeve glanced over her shoulder more than once to be sure she wasn't followed. Her expression was not the serene one I've grown accustomed to; instead it was twisted and frustrated, but with a determined bent. Her steps were strong, as if she knew exactly where she was headed.

And that is all. The owl lost interest after that, and her thoughts only consist of her chicks and her mate.

I shiver. Judging by Maeve's sudden change in behavior, I'm more certain than ever that she is possessed by the body walker. Her demeanor seems more like Ida's than her own.

*She went this way.* I point toward the left fork in the path.

Sebastian doesn't question me. He knows I have ways of obtaining information that are beyond what others can do. The owl hoots a goodbye behind us, making Sebastian jump, but I keep him from straying off the path. My teeth are set on edge, clenched together, and I'm praying we find Maeve before it's too late.

*What do you think Ida wants us for?* Sebastian thinks.

I shudder. *I don't know. Power, like Lady Aisling, maybe? I've heard her thoughts, and she clearly covets our talents.*

Until now, I've tried to chalk up all our encounters with the body walker to coincidence. But every one of them has been connected to us in some way, and Ida has been close by for them all. First, the nice woman who let me have the last of the day's flowers and her husband in the market. Then Jemma, Euna, and now Maeve. She's been circling us, getting ever closer, waiting for the right time to strike so she can use us like Lady Aisling. No wonder she had such a keen interest in learning more about the Lady's garden!

The sheer horror of that thought nearly stops me in my tracks. And it probably would've made me turn around if we were going after anyone but Maeve.

If Ida did take her, it was because of us. How can we

abandon her to the same fate we had? We're probably walking into a trap, but we can't stomach leaving her behind.

The moon above provides some light as it trickles down through the trees. Even so, we still stumble over the occasional root and rock. The going is slow, and sometimes I pause to consult with the animals to see if they recall Maeve passing the night before. Thank goodness we were able to escape the Archives so quickly! Animals' memories are not long, and if we'd had to wait another day or two, they would've already forgotten.

The result is a circuitous path around the mountains, almost as though the body walker either didn't know where they were headed or didn't want to be followed. Exhaustion begins to wear at my determination and focus. The moon is directly overhead now, its beams streaking between the branches to illuminate bushes and flowers and bark and odd leaves, all of which try to distract me from the task at hand. But Sebastian keeps me grounded, calling me back when my feet begin to stray. Our progress slows until we find ourselves in front of the yawning black mouth of a cave. Fireflies dance in front of the entrance, making it seem both deadly and inviting. I reach out to catch one in my hands, but Sebastian's words stop me cold.

"Look! Footprints." He points to a boot mark left in the mud at the entrance to the cave.

"It could easily belong to Maeve or Ida," I say. "It's not alone either."

The mud at the entrance is littered with tracks in various sizes. My spine goes rigid, and all trace of sleep falls away as though someone threw a bucket of ice over my head.

This is it. We've found the body walker's lair.

One glance at Sebastian's face makes it clear he understands this all too well.

I pull two candles out of my bag and light them with a match to keep the darkness at bay. Then I hand one to Sebastian. *Are you ready?*

He takes the candle and twines the fingers of his free hand with mine. *As I'll ever be.*

We press onward into the cave, leaving the moonlit forest behind. The walls are damp to the touch and coated with moss, making the floors slippery. But there are also fresh footprints left by Maeve and Ida. All we have to do is follow them when confronted with a choice of tunnels. In a few places, the going is steep and rocky, but we manage as best we can.

Then the tunnel begins to widen until we stand at the mouth of a huge cavern full of stalactites and stalagmites on one side, which taper off to a giant pool on the far side of the cavern.

On the bank of the pool stands Maeve.

I reach out with my mind, but I don't sense Ida anywhere in the cavern, or nearby out of sight. My talent wanders all the way back to the entrance, but I can't find any trace of her. She must have stepped out, perhaps for more provisions or to return to the library with some sort of cover story. Or maybe she's out hunting *us*. Whatever the reason, she isn't here, and that is good news.

But still we must be cautious. We flatten against the moss-covered cave wall and peek around the corner. Maeve can't see us, but we can just make out her expression. It isn't what I expected, but it is what I feared. She looks angry and frustrated, just as Jemma did when the body walker had her under their control. If Maeve were free, she'd be running for the exits to return to us, I have no doubt. At the very least, she'd look bewildered.

I let my talent reach into Maeve's mind to confirm what I already know.

But this time I don't find what I'm looking for.

I stand at the edge of the cavern in shocked confusion. Horror trickles upward, working its way from my toes until it reaches the reeling, panicked thoughts in my brain. I sink to the ground.

I can't feel Ida's mind in Maeve's head. There's no hint of her own consciousness being shoved aside as I've seen and experienced myself so many times.

There's only her. Just *her*.

"She's the body walker," I whisper, hardly able to believe it. Then I clap my hand over my mouth.

*What?* Sebastian thinks.

*Maeve. It's not Ida; it's Maeve.*

Only one mind resides in Maeve's head—one I know and love. I had no idea until now that it's also the one that haunts our nightmares.

Sebastian pales, his dark hair casting his eyes in shadows and making his scar a stark white line. *You must be mistaken. It can't be. It must be Ida.*

I shakily regain my feet. *No mistake. I was wrong before. It's Maeve. It's been her all along.*

His shocked silence is a stark contrast to the whirling confusion in his brain. *That means Maeve is the one who took over Jemma. How could she do that? And then pretend to be our friend?*

Tears burn the backs of my eyes. How could I have not known? Why couldn't I tell? Perhaps it's because I've only felt the effects of the body walking talent in use and never before the mind actually wielding it. Indeed, as I send my talent deeper into the cave, the shape of Maeve's mind doesn't feel like the victims I've seen. But every once and a while, there's a sickly flare of something familiar...

She's using her talent on someone. That's it. That's why it escaped my notice. She didn't use it around us. She must have been careful ever since I told her I was a mind reader.

But who is she using it on? For a moment, I hope it's Jemma, but I find no trace of her in the cave. If she's here, she must be so far gone that she's no longer struggling and I can't sense her. Maybe that's what happened to Ida too. But there are others. They're screaming for help.

And I know them.

My insides have gone hollow, and my knees weaken. Sebastian is right next to me, quaking like a leaf in storm.

*What now? What's wrong? Simone, I'm too scared to even say a word aloud anymore.*

*She has Lady Aisling's other shells. Our friends.* Kalia, the dream eater. Natasha, the illusion crafter, Elias, the thought thrower, and Melanthe, the mind mover. I'm relieved she doesn't have Finn as far as I can tell. He's a mind changer and is deceptively dangerous.

Sebastian frowns. *But what is she doing with them?*

I shudder, recalling my earlier thoughts. *They're damaged like us. She must want to use them like Lady Aisling did.*

Sebastian's face shifts from horror to determination faster than I've ever seen it. *We can't let her do that. We have to stop her.*

In that we're of one mind. It's one thing to betray us. It's another to kidnap our friends who've only just been reunited with their families in order to use them too.

We have no choice but to help them.

# CHAPTER TWENTY

We decide that we'll confront Maeve together. We lend each other our courage, what little of it we have left.

Cautiously, we clamber down from the top of the cavern opening. The threshold is rocky and sharp, and I flinch at every noise we make. I'm surprised Maeve doesn't hear us coming. Her focus and concentration must be divided elsewhere. It's a tiny bit of luck, but we'll happily take it.

When we're about ten paces away, I call out. "Maeve?"

Half of me hopes I'm wrong, and when she turns around, she'll be overtaken by the body walker—someone who isn't her. The other half of me aches with the heavy burden of the truth.

She whirls at my voice, surprise written all over her face.

"Simone? Sebastian?" Then her expression settles. "You followed me."

"We did," I say. "We thought the body walker had captured you. We wanted to help." A sudden lump forms in my throat.

She raises her eyebrows. "You thought the body walker had me?" She moves toward us, and we unconsciously take a step back. "What's this now?"

"We know," Sebastian squeaks.

"Know what?" Maeve says.

She reaches for him, and Sebastian shrinks back. She frowns, then laughs. "What is the matter with you?"

"Why?" I breathe out the word softly, yet it still manages to echo off the walls of the cavern.

"Why what? Simone, what is going on?" Maeve places her hands on her hips, and for one moment she seems just like she always has. But I dip into her mind, prying deeper than usual. Her determination that I attributed to wanting to find out what happened to her family has warped into something darker. Her fierceness that I chalked up to loyalty has taken on a cutting edge.

But before I can delve too deeply, her thoughts calm and smooth over. I cannot see beneath them anymore. She knows how to conceal things from me, and that realization shocks me.

Maeve's mind has always been orderly. I never knew that was because she had so much to hide.

"We know what you are." I choke out. Speaking the words is a physically painful thing.

She folds her arms across her chest. "What are you talking about?"

"You're the body walker. You're the one who took over Euna. You took over Sebastian's sister, Jemma. You probably took Ida too."

"Where is Jemma?" he whispers. "What did you do with her? Why hasn't she met us here yet?"

A look of innocence crosses her face. "That's absurd. You're just confused. I'd never do that. You know me better. I've protected you both, cared for you when there was no one else to help you."

I think back to the time we met Maeve and recall encountering the confused man lost in the woods and the strangeness of the empty, yet recently used shack. She must've taken him over and abandoned him far enough away to be so lost that she could use his home herself for a little while. And then we happened upon her.

Did she know from the very start what Sebastian and I were? That we were talented? A sick feeling worms its way over my body.

"You never cared for us. You only wanted to use us. Just like everyone else." Tears burn my eyes.

Maeve sighs sympathetically. "Oh, Simone, this is just the aftereffects of what Lady Aisling did to you. You're confused. I will help you make sense of it." She reaches out a hand, and I flinch.

"Don't touch me. I know you have others here in this cave somewhere. Friends of ours from our time with the Lady. They're under your control."

Sebastian's eyes are wide and watery, and his hands ball into fists at his side. "You're no better than she is."

Now it's Maeve's turn to flinch. "As bad as Lady Aisling? That demon who kept hundreds of talented people imprisoned for decades? That is too harsh. And far off the mark." She huffs, all pretense dropped.

She begins to pace by the edge of the water. "I won't lie

to you further. I'm telling the truth when I say I care for you both. I swear to that." She drops her arms to her sides. "Lady Aisling stole me away from my family, from my husband and children. They're long dead, and I only got a few precious years with them. I want them back. I've been searching for a soul summoner to take them under my wing and use their talent to bring my children back to me. I just needed the right vessels. The children Lady Aisling already damaged are perfect for it."

My skin crawls. "You want to use them as hosts for your own children's souls?"

"But what will happen to our friends?" Sebastian says. His hand is tightly wrapped around mine.

"If you're going to fill up a jug of water with wine, you must first pour the water out," Maeve says simply.

Shock roils over me yet again. "You'll kill them."

"No. Just release their souls from their bodies."

"Where will *they* go? Do you have hosts lined up for them?"

Maeve frowns. "Why would I do that? I don't care what happens to them. I only need their bodies to give to my children."

"But you only had three children. Can't you release at least one of our friends?" Sebastian pleads.

She shakes her head. "Not until my task is complete. Your friends are useful, I'll give them that. And what Lady Aisling did to them makes them easier to control than your average person. I need them."

"Didn't your children already live full lives long ago?" I ask. "How do you know they'll even want to come back?"

Confusion crosses Maeve's face. "Of course they do. They have to. We were family."

Her words are a knife to my gut. For a time I thought she might be a stand-in for my own. Now I'm horrified I was blind to what she really is.

"How do you know?" Sebastian presses. Like me, hope lingers in his heart that maybe we can reason with her, maybe we can convince her to return and be the kind woman we believed her to be.

"Because they died," Maeve spits out. "Not long after Lady Aisling stole me away. My two girls and a little boy. I've discovered that much about what happened to them. I won't rest until we're reunited."

"I'm sorry," I say. And I am. I know what it feels like to lose your entire family. "But what about our friends' families? They just got them back. Our friends aren't yours to take." My hands ball into fists at my side.

Maeve's face twists. "*Everything* has been taken from me. Why shouldn't I take a little something back?"

"Why does it have to be from the comet-blessed? Why not someone else? You took Jemma and Ida too. Why not someone like them?" I'm getting desperate, and while it's not the best argument, it's the only one I can think of at the moment.

"I used Jemma because she was convenient, and I was looking for Lady Aisling's shells. Ida was just too nosy and got in the way. Now they're both off doing my bidding and taking supplies from the nearest village." Maeve shakes her head. "The comet-blessed, specifically those with mind-based talents, are the best vessels. I've done my research. If there were a better way to bring my children back, I'd do it."

Shock resonates through me for the millionth time tonight. *That* is what she was researching. The soul summoner. Their powers and how to use them. *She* must've stolen that journal from Connor. And, like it or not, we helped her.

*Simone, I want to leave before she gets any ideas about using us.* Sebastian's thoughts echo my own fears. *We should tell Rachel and the other librarians that Maeve has Ida and Jemma. Maybe they can help us get them free. This is too much for us to handle on our own.*

As much as I hate to admit it, he's right. We came here expecting to rescue Maeve and have an ally in her as we escaped. We had no idea the body walker had so many people stowed here under her command. *Move slowly, then run.*

We begin to back away while Maeve continues babbling about soul summoners. Then we break into a run. But before we can reach the exit to the cavern, figures appear from all sides.

The other shells, Lady Aisling's hollow dolls, just like us. My heart sinks at their vacant eyes. They're under Maeve's control right now. One brush against their thoughts, and the sickly feeling of the body walker—of Maeve—using them digs into me. Their minds beg for help, rising as they see me, then growing fainter as Maeve tightens her grip.

*Be careful,* I warn Sebastian. He knows the dangers of our friends' powers as well as I do.

We duck and dodge through the stalagmites, avoiding the all-too-realistic illusions that Natasha throws at us. Elias uses his ability to throw thoughts to confuse us by imitating my voice in Sebastian's head and his in mine. But I know Sebastian well enough to be able to differentiate between things he'd really say and those he would not. Still, it's harder than I expected. I've never been on the receiving end of Elias's talent before. We were friends, but we kept out of each other's heads when we had our bodies to ourselves. It only seemed right. But now…

Suddenly Sebastian is knocked flat, struck on the shoulder by a rock, probably flung by Melanthe, though I can't see her from where I'm standing. The chain on Sebastian's necklace, old and brittle, snaps and the obsidian arrowhead slips out of his reach. I try to get to him, but Kalia blocks my path. She's older than me and bigger; I could never hope to force my way past her. Sebastian scrambles to his feet, desperately casting around for the arrowhead. It landed not far from me, and I might be able to throw it back to him if I can find it in the darkness of the cavern.

*Simone! Where is it? Do you see it?* His frantic cries resound in my head.

*It's here! I'll get it to you!* I dive for the talisman, but no sooner do I get my hands on it than Sebastian's pleas cease. Maeve stands next to him with her hand on his shoulder.

I'm terrified to look in his mind for fear of what I might find.

I cling to the arrowhead for dear life as I send my talent toward my friend who now gazes at me blankly.

*Hello, Simone*, Maeve says inside Sebastian's head. I let out a wail, then quickly shove the arrowhead in my pocket.

I must not be captured. I must leave here and get help. Almost every friend I've ever had is in this cavern and under a body walker's control.

And I've just become their only hope for freedom.

I run headlong through the stalagmites, then down the tunnels. I don't stop running until I can see the moon overhead and the stars glimmering above.

# CHAPTER TWENTY-ONE

I race headlong through the woods, heading—I hope—in the direction of the Archives. Tears stream over my cheeks. I can't believe I had to leave Sebastian. My best friend. I don't think I'll ever be able to forget the terror in his head and heart just before Maeve took him over.

Her betrayal is nothing if not complete.

My steps begin to slow, but I can feel the press of many minds ahead. The library must be nearby. I just have to go a little farther. The only question is: Will I really be safe there? Will they welcome me back? I lost Sebastian. It's my fault—I'm the one who insisted we go. He didn't even want to, but he took the risk for me. So I wouldn't have to face the body walker alone.

And now I've left him behind, his greatest fear realized.

I swallow the rocks in my throat, even as my feet falter. I catch myself, and when I glance up again, I can see the gray stones of the Parillan Archives between the trees. A new burst of energy fills me, even though I know Lady Aisling's other hollow dolls are far behind. When I reach the imposing front door, I bang on the wooden planks as though my life depends on it. To my relief, Rachel opens the door. I throw my arms around her waist and begin to cry.

Rachel puts an arm around me as she locks the door behind us. "What's the matter? What happened?" She frowns. "Where's Sebastian?"

When I begin to cry harder, sobs racking my shoulders, she understands without words. "Oh dear... Come, you're safe now."

She picks me up and carries me back to my quarters, but she doesn't leave. She sets me on the bed and hands me a kerchief, then settles into the chair nearby.

"When you're ready, tell me everything."

And I do. I don't leave anything out. Not how we took the obsidian, not Maeve's true nature, not that Ida and Jemma are nearby, not even our old friends, the other shells. When I finish, Rachel's skin has taken on a sickly green tinge.

"You're certain Maeve really is the body walker?"

I nod. "I wish I was wrong. More than anything."

Rachel gives me a sad smile. "Of course you do. It was clear how attached you and Sebastian had become to her." She shakes her head, her expression hardening. "What a terrible woman. And to take Jemma and Ida too. We'll help Sebastian and get all of them back. Even if Euna says no to officially helping, I'll do it anyway. It isn't right. You've already been through so much."

"Thank you," I say.

Rachel leaves to let me rest while she informs Euna of all I've told her.

I remain still, curled up on the bed, haunted by my circling thoughts. I failed my best friend. Now, I really have no one. Eventually I fall into a dreamless sleep.

When Rachel returns the next morning, she tells me that Euna is glad I'm back and has tasked Rachel with finding a way to save Sebastian, his sister, and Ida and to stop Maeve's plans. I'm so relieved I could cry all over again. The first thing we do is head for the stacks. Rachel believes there might be more about body walkers in some of the older documents that we haven't searched yet.

When we get to the first level of the library, though, I pause. "Rachel? Can we go in here first?"

"Of course. What do you need?"

"I just wanted to see Maeve's research desk." She collected numerous texts over the last few weeks and kept them on a particular desk on this level. There might be something in her papers that would give a clue to how she plans to find the soul summoner.

"Good idea," Rachel says. When we reach the alcove with Maeve's desk, we're startled to find Connor shuffling through her papers.

Rachel puts her hands on her hips. "Do you need something?"

He whirls around with a guilty expression on his face. "Oh, I... No, I just thought I saw something of mine here, but I was mistaken."

I frown, not trusting him. I don't feel even a little guilty when I peek into his mind as he ducks away.

*I could have sworn I saw her with that journal in her hand*

*the other day, even though she denied it. Maybe she hid it somewhere.*
*No respect…*

Before, I couldn't have imagined why Maeve would want to steal Connor's research, nor why he would ever suspect that. But after hearing his conversation with Devynne and knowing what I do about Maeve's plans for the soul summoner, I have no doubt his suspicions are well founded.

"Did you want to look at her things?" Rachel asks me, bringing me back to the task at hand. I'd gotten sidetracked staring after Connor this time.

"Yes, please."

I begin to sort through them, recognizing some of the books as ones Maeve pored over quite thoroughly. I set those aside, and Rachel begins to scan through them for any mention of a soul summoner. As I shuffle books around, something slips out and falls on the chair—a map. Curious, I unfold the sheet of parchment and spread it out on the desk. Shock ripples through me.

This is *my* map. Or rather, the map of Parilla Rachel used to determine that the village of Wren is now underwater. She even updated it using her book binding talent with a notation of where Wren was once located.

A heady mix of emotions tumbles through me. Did Maeve save this because she thought I'd want it? Did she do it to help me, because she really cared for me? Or is there some other reason? Something I can't see yet that would help her find the soul summoner? I wish terribly for it to be the first, but I suspect it's really the latter.

"Strange that she would hold on to that." Rachel says over my shoulder.

"I thought so too," I say.

"Why don't you keep it safe. Just in case there's more there than we realize." Rachel folds it up and tucks it into my bag. "And you know, I think you should probably hold on to those obsidian artifacts too." I'd intended to return them while we were here in the library. "If Maeve decides she wants you too, they ought to keep you safe from her talent."

My eyes widen. "Are you sure it's all right? I feel terrible that we took them and had to break that glass case, but we didn't see any other way at the time."

"You did what you thought was best and right. And you brought them back. You're more valuable to Maeve than any of the others here. If anyone needs the protection, it's you."

My heart sinks. No, the one who *really* needed it was Sebastian.

"I'll bring them back again once this is all over."

Rachel squeezes my shoulder. "I know you will." Her hand drops back to her side. "Well, I think we've exhausted this avenue. Let's go upstairs to the older documents, shall we?"

I agree. The journal doesn't appear to be in Maeve's desk. She must've taken it with her.

As we head up the stairs, I can't help but feel as though eyes follow me. I brush the feeling off, and it isn't long before we're settled in the oldest part of the library. The dust makes me sneeze, but I pore over everything Rachel sets in front of me, trying hard to remain focused on the task at hand.

All we know right now is that the last recorded soul summoner disappeared long, long ago. In a way, that's a relief. Maeve's plan really is just a wild-goose chase if she can't find a living soul summoner. The afternoon passes in a hazy daze of dust and words. They seem to float off the page and dance before my eyes until they hardly even make sense anymore. But Rachel has no issues with that. She is as studious as ever, and just before dinner-time, she lets out a little cry over what looks like a town record.

"Simone," Rachel says, her face drawn tight and serious. "Come here."

I sit next to her on the bench and look over her shoulder. "What is it?"

"This document… It's very badly labeled. You can barely read it anymore." She shows me the top of the scroll. Where the town name ought to be is just a smudge of ink that looks like it got wet. "I think it's from your village. From Wren."

My skin grows cold all of sudden. "Are you sure?"

She sighs. "Listen to this. It might shed light on both your and Maeve's predicaments."

*Our town has been particularly blessed by the Comet. At least a dozen of the children here are talented, and several of the previous generation too. But today our numbers have been reduced by a great tragedy. A strange, wealthy woman arrived in town last week with an entourage. We were honored to host her, and she delighted the local shopkeepers by spending liberally on their wares. But she was not what we thought. And now she has stolen more from us than can ever be repaid.*

*The lady, as we have now discovered, has a rare talent: magic eating. She and her servants kidnapped every talented man, woman, and child in Wren, except a handful who were traveling abroad while she was here (our soul summoner, gift giver, and one of our water wishers are, thankfully, safe). Those who pursued her have either disappeared or have not returned the same. Families have been destroyed, and we will not forget this terrible wrong. The names of those who were stolen are recorded below:*

*Rati Alberg, spot hopper*

*Romana M. Casares, body walker*

*Simone Casares, mind reader*

*Kenyatta Combs, green grower*

*Emilian R. Corallo, skin saver*

*Jerod A. Dada, color changer*

*Neri Frieden, shape shifter*

*Zona Futrell, water wisher*

*Malvin A. Gaccione, book binder*

*Catarina L. Heilbert, green grower*

*Doros Hooley, scent sower*

*Darci Kassin, wind whistler*

*Glynae Pellerito, frost finder*

*Bochim Starek, wind whistler*

*Riley J. Wetherill, earth rattler*

My hand freezes over my own name on the list—and that of my mother. She was a body walker.

Shock electrifies the blood in my veins. Impossible. I could never have been related to a monster who uses people.

"This can't be a coincidence," Rachel says, the excitement of discovery making her cheeks flush.

I frown, suddenly repulsed by the scroll. "What do you mean?"

"Your mother's middle name. It begins with an *M*."

An odd feeling curls inside me as if I'm spinning out of control, even though I'm not moving an inch.

"I don't remember what the *M* stands for. It wasn't in the note I wrote to be sure I didn't forget," I say more to myself than Rachel.

"It has to be Maeve," Rachel says. "But neither of you remember the other, because Lady Aisling used Sebastian's talent to remove your memories of your previous lives. All that you kept was that there was a family you'd lost."

"And that we wanted that family back." My hands begin to shake, and soon the quiver ripples over my entire body. "Until last night, I never even had a clue that Maeve was talented!"

And yet, it makes a terrible sort of sense. The Lady was able to successfully transform Maeve into one of the flowers in her garden, but my mind-based talent prevented her from doing the same to me. Instead, the Lady used my own mother's talent to enslave me.

It's horrifying. Sickening. And the sort of thing Lady Aisling would have taken particular pleasure in.

I wrap my arms around my middle and rest my cheek on the desk. It feels as though the breath has been yanked from my lungs.

No wonder we bonded so quickly, Maeve and me. Some unconscious part of us must have recognized the other. And given the powerful spells performed on us both by the Lady's life bringer and youth keeper talents, we've barely aged a day since we were abducted.

*Maeve is my mother.* I think it again and again, trying to stun myself into believing it's truly real.

It is. In my heart, I know it without a doubt.

What I haven't figured out yet is what I'm going to do about it.

# CHAPTER TWENTY-TWO

Rachel and I spend the rest of the day making plans to rescue Sebastian. Euna, however, has instructed Rachel to keep me here. But Rachel has promised she'll find a way around it. I've read her thoughts, so I know it's true. She doesn't think it's fair to keep me from my friend, and she knows my talent will be necessary to the success of our plans.

When night falls, we sneak out of the library. Despite Euna's order to keep me safely hidden inside, Rachel has found a way to smuggle me out of the fortress.

"Quickly," she whispers as she cracks open the door to my quarters. I've been pacing my room for the last hour, dressed and ready to go, unable to focus on anything else. I waste no time obeying. She's prepared with a laundry cart and several large wicker bins. She opens the top of one—it's empty aside from Rachel's cloak and satchel. I climb inside and nestle next to them.

She wheels me through the halls and down the ramp that leads to the room where they employ washerwomen to clean the clothes of the librarians and researchers. It's late enough that there's no one there now, which means we can slip out through the back door of the Archives with no one the wiser.

Rachel parks the cart and opens the bin where I'm hiding. There are two more carts just like hers right next to it. She helps me climb out, but stops me before opening the back door. "Can you make sure no one's out there? You can do that, can't you? Feel the presence of nearby minds?"

I send my talent searching just beyond the door and into the forest surrounding it.

"Only the nighttime animals."

"Perfect."

We sneak out, closing the door carefully behind us, then hurry into the woods. One of the obsidian artifacts is hung around my neck, and the rest are safely tucked away in my bag.

Rachel borrowed an obsidian ring she found in the library to keep herself safe too.

I retrace my steps from the night before, the path burned into my brain after the stress of my flight home. It isn't long before we reach the cave, and my heart takes a seat in my throat.

This time, I'm better prepared. This time, I know so much more. I just don't know how I'm going to balance what Maeve is with what she's become to me. Perhaps if I tell her the truth, she will stop her plan. But it also might make her more desperate to get our other family members back. And she'd definitely come after me to keep me with her. At least, that's what Rachel believes, and I can't deny it makes sense.

We're both desperate to regain what was stolen from us. We just had no idea it was each other.

The cave entrance comes into view. A slit in the mountainside, half-hidden by hanging vines. I can feel Maeve inside the cave, along with the faint trace of a few other minds endlessly calling for help. My old friends, stolen again to be used against anyone who stands in her way. For a moment, I even catch a hint of Jemma and Ida's minds before they're shoved too far down for my talent to reach.

Maeve must be stopped. Even if she is my mother.

I can make out a few of the words in Maeve's mind, but none of them are useful. Her mind is so structured and orderly that she's able to conceal things from me. She probably learned how to keep her private thoughts to herself raising me. I thought it odd before, but now it makes perfect sense.

"She's definitely in there, along with Jemma and Ida, and so are the others with mind-based talents I told you about. Under her control, they're dangerous. But usually they're my friends." I frown. I've never been at odds with them before, particularly Sebastian. Just the thought is foreign and strange, almost like saying my own arm could be used against me. Unthinkable.

Rachel puts a comforting hand on my back. "We'll get Sebastian safely away, and then we'll see what we can do about your other friends."

"Yes, Sebastian first." It's my fault he was captured. I need to fix this.

We push aside the vines and enter the cave, keeping our footsteps soft and candles aloft. But we quickly discover that Maeve has prepared for intruders. We've barely gone two yards into the dark tunnel when a terrible roar echoes through the corridor.

Rachel's voice quivers. "Are you sure there isn't anything else here in the caves?"

"Positive," I say.

"What do you sense now?"

Before I can respond, a dark shadow blocks the path up ahead and the sound resonates again, making my hair stand on end. The shape coalesces into the form of a giant snakelike beast, with a horned head and gaping mouth filled with row upon row of wicked-looking teeth.

Rachel screams and stumbles back, but I begin to laugh. "Don't be afraid. That's just Natasha."

My companion's expression is shocked. "You know this monster?"

"No, but I do know the person who created this *illusion* of a monster. Natasha is an illusion crafter. She can make illusions of both sight and sound, just not touch. It may look and sound fierce, but really it's nothing at all. She used to entertain us with her talent when the Lady wasn't using us."

Rachel looks back and forth between me and the menacing beast as it inches closer and closer. "This is an illusion? You're absolutely certain?"

"Definitely. If it was real, I'd be able to sense its mind. There's nothing there." I walk straight up to the beast and stick my hand right where its snout appears to be.

Nothing but dead air.

Rachel still looks uneasy, but she inches forward around the beast. When it lunges at her a second time, she manages not to scream.

It roars as we pass it by. I wonder if Natasha can sense what her illusions do when she's not nearby. If the roaring echoed back to them, that alone would give our presence away. This is an alarm for Maeve to know someone has entered her domain.

And we just set it off.

"That's quite a talent," Rachel mutters, and I snort.

"Wait until you see Melanthe's. Now *she's* actually dangerous."

Rachel's brows knit. "What can she do?"

"Move things with her mind."

"Anything?"

"Anything that isn't tied down. We definitely need to watch out for her."

"Now that's one talent I'd prefer to have on our side."

I laugh again, despite the circumstances. I like Rachel. She's funny and doesn't treat me like I can't understand simply because I'm younger or smaller than everyone else. She takes me seriously. That I appreciate the most. I wish *she* was my mother, not a monstrous body walker.

And Lady Aisling knew all along. *This* is what she meant when I visited her. She told me if I ever discovered who the body walker is, I'd regret it. I hadn't understood at the time. In fact, I brushed it off and had all but forgotten about it until now.

Even without her powers, the Lady still delights in finding new ways to hurt other comet-blessed people. She was right; I do regret it. And somehow that makes everything worse.

Rachel taps me on the shoulder, pulling me out of my reverie. "Is that an illusion too?"

A huge crevasse yawns in front of us, far too wide to jump across. I peer into the abyss and see that way, way down, are more stalagmites. From here, they look small enough to be splinters, but I know they're probably humongous up close. I take a step back, frowning.

"This wasn't here last night…" I murmur. "It must be an illusion."

Rachel shudders. "It's a very convincing one."

"Natasha's craft *is* excellent."

I take a deep breath and begin to step forward, but Rachel yanks me back.

She eyes the gulf suspiciously. "I don't think it's safe to assume this is an illusion. What if Maeve has another talent in her possession? Like an earth rattler. Or maybe you took a different path to the cavern with the pool."

I hadn't thought of that, but those are both good points.

"I'm almost certain this is the route we took," I say. "But let's test it just in case."

I grab a loose rock nearby, then toss it into the gulf. It quickly disappears, but makes a thud much faster than it would hitting the bottom.

"Where did it go?" Rachel says.

"The illusion swallowed it up. See? Nothing to worry about." Before she can stop me, I step out onto the illusion-covered path. She squeaks, then stops as she realizes it looks as though I'm suspended over thin air. She swallows hard.

"It'll be easier if you close your eyes," I say, reaching out my hand.

She smiles weakly. "And here I thought I was supposed to be helping you." She squeezes her eyes shut and shuffles one foot forward so she can feel the ground under her feet. Then she grabs my hand tightly. "Just tell me when we're on the other side."

We make slow progress as she shuffles her way across. I can't help but admire Natasha's work. She really is an artist.

When we're finally free of the illusion, I let go of Rachel's hand. "We're clear now."

She sneaks an eye open and breathes out in relief. "That isn't a thing I want to do again anytime soon."

I can't help but laugh, then clap my hand over my mouth. I send my thoughts into her head.

*We need to be careful to remain quiet now. We can talk like this, if you don't mind.*

Rachel's eyes widen. *You mean you can hear my thoughts now too?* I nod, and she considers for a moment. *All right. Yes, that's probably wise.*

We continue down the tunnel, hugging the walls just in case. And we keep an eye out for any other traps or illusions. Before long, we reach the end of the tunnel where it leads into the cavernous room where Sebastian and I found Maeve last night. Right now it's empty, but when I stretch out my talent, I can feel the shape of several minds hidden in other small caves off this one. That's where she's keeping Jemma and Ida and the other shells.

*They're not far*, I think to Rachel.

*It's a trap then*, she thinks.

*Seems likely.*

*Is Sebastian here?*

My heart throbs in my throat. *Yes.*

We hang back for a few minutes, waiting for something to happen. I know Elias is nearby and close to Maeve, which means he can probably feel our minds with his thought throwing talent.

*Where's Sebastian?* Rachel asks.

I concentrate until I feel the faint yell of Sebastian's mind. Maeve has him under her control, but he's resisting and screaming inside as much as he can. Tears burn my eyes. He's terrified.

*He's in a cave just beyond the pool.*

Rachel frowns. *That will make getting to him tricky. Is there another way around?*

I shake my head. *Not that we saw last time, but maybe?*

We retrace our steps to the last fork in the tunnels in the

hope of finding another way to get to Sebastian. But all we find are dead ends. Disheartened, we return to the main tunnel and the entrance to the cavern.

A new idea occurs to me, and while I feel confident it will work, it scares me. But I must try it. No matter how much it would scare Sebastian, I know he'd do the same for me if the roles were reversed. How many times has he gone along with my silly ideas, even when he was terrified by them, just so I wouldn't have to be alone?

Determination floods every inch of my body, and I know deep in my bones that this is the way.

I quickly fill in Rachel, and while she isn't thrilled with the risks, she has no choice but to agree that it's a sound plan.

*Be careful*, she says as I step into the cavern.

*I'll try.*

I've barely gone two yards when a rock flies at my body. I drop to the ground, then roll as another projectile heads my way.

I scramble to my feet, only to have to duck once again. Instead of heading for Sebastian, I make a beeline toward where I sensed Maeve and Elias hiding in a cave offshoot. Hopefully, that will throw them off their game and draw their fire while

Rachel can free Sebastian and get him to safety. I'm banking on Maeve's affection to prevent her from harming me, though I worry that may be a longer shot than I'd like.

As I stumble between the stalagmites, my other friends appear at cave openings around the cavern. I already knew where they were, so this is no surprise, but the mirrored menacing looks on their faces is still unsettling.

"What are you trying to accomplish, Simone?" All four of them speak in unison, which makes me shudder.

"I just want to talk," I say, warily keeping an eye on the approaching shells. They get closer with every breath. Even the way they frown reminds me of the look I've seen fleetingly on Maeve's face over the last few weeks. My poor friends are just dolls lolling on strings.

The worst part is that I can hear their own voices too. Far away and faint, but panicked.

*Simone! Help!*

Once, when we were Lady Aisling's captives, we each reached a point where we gave up. We stopped fighting and had no choice but to accept that being controlled was a new normal.

But now we've had a taste of freedom. We know that isn't normal. It's a violation of the worst kind.

And we'll do anything to get that freedom back.

I don't know how I can help them now—freeing Sebastian will be tricky enough—but eventually I must find a way. I can't abandon them to Maeve's whims.

"And what do you wish to talk about?" Maeve's own voice echoes off the stalagmites and stalactites in the huge cavern, her servants suddenly silent.

I steel my nerves. I've made up my mind to tell her the truth. I expect to fail, but hope to succeed. The other shells have converged, and Maeve uses their arms to usher me to the side cave where she waits. From the corner of my eye, I see the edge of Rachel's cloak as she and Sebastian cross the entrance to the tunnel that will lead them to freedom.

*Run!* I think toward them both. Sebastian's mind is foggy, but now that the obsidian arrowhead is back around his neck, it's beginning to clear. *Get to safety. Don't wait for me. I'll follow when I can.*

*Simone?* Sebastian thinks groggily. *What are you doing? Go with Rachel. I'll be right behind you.*

We both know it's a lie, but he obeys anyway. They better hurry. Maeve is distracted for now, but it won't be long before she realizes her connection to Sebastian has been severed.

He needs to be far away when that happens.

# CHAPTER TWENTY-THREE

The shells drag me into Maeve's cave, and I blink rapidly. It's brighter here. Maeve has a warm fire burning, lending more light than the candles in the main cavern. It looks like there's a natural vent in here too. And then there's Maeve. Her auburn hair falling prettily over her shoulders, conflicting with the terrible smile she now wears.

"I'm glad you came back, Simone. You know how much I like you. You'll make a perfect vessel."

A shiver runs down my spine. Despite her profession of caring for me, she would still use me. Telling her that I'm really her daughter is the only way I might be able to shock some sense back into her.

And prevent her from using me as a shell.

The others have a fierce grip on my arms, thanks to Maeve's controls. "You don't need to hold so tightly," I say. "Even if I tried to run away, you'd catch me again in seconds."

Maeve laughs. "Do you think I'm that easy to fool?"

I shrug, though that's harder than I expected with four sets of hands weighing my arms down. "No. It's just that I know you don't want to harm me. Not really. And I'm not going to run away." Not until I've at least figured out a way to save Jemma, if not Ida and the other shells too.

Maeve raises an eyebrow. "You're right. I don't wish to harm you. I could have taken control of you at any time, but I never did, now did I? And I still won't. But why should I believe you won't run away?"

I bite my lip. I'm not entirely sure how she'll react to the news I bring.

"Have you found the soul summoner you need to use them as vessels?" I nod at my friends, though the implication is nauseating.

Maeve's smile falters. "Not yet. But soon. I know where they were last. It's just a matter of determining where they are now."

While she speaks, I stretch my talent out, searching the tunnels to see if Sebastian and Rachel are clear yet. To my relief, they're already on the path through the woods, hurrying back to the library.

"Where do you think that is?" I ask.

A coy glint sparkles in Maeve's eyes. She opens her mouth to speak, but her face suddenly falls. Her expression shifts into something new.

"What have you done? Where is he? Why can't I sense him? How did you get to him?" she sputters.

I straighten my spine and tilt my head up, letting my ghostly hair fall back from my face. "You're not our only friend." I don't mention that he has obsidian protecting him now. If she doesn't know what the black stone can do, I don't want to give that away.

Her expression hardens. "It was a librarian then." Her fists clench. "I bet it was Rachel. She always was a bit too fond of you. Maybe I should have taken her instead of Ida."

All of a sudden, my friends release me and march single file into the cavern. She's sending them after Sebastian and Rachel.

"Wait!" I cry. "Let him go. You don't need him. Let him go, and I'll stay. I promise. I won't try to run away." The most terrifying thing about those words is that I mean them. Maeve is my mother, the one person I've wanted to find ever since I can remember. While she isn't at all what I expected, leaving her is not so simple now that I've found her.

I'm her daughter. I may be the only one who can reach her. The only one who can stop her. What she's doing is wrong—horribly wrong—but she's doing it out of grief and desperation. That I can understand.

I peek inside her head, and while her thoughts are still well concealed, they're also confused. "Why would you do that?" Suspicion begins to brew. I need to put a stop to that immediately.

"Because I'm your daughter."

The other shells halt their march, frozen in place waiting for commands. Confusion reigns in Maeve's head.

"But that's…that's not possible," she says, though I can see from her thoughts that part of her hopes it's true.

I nod vehemently. "It *is* true. I swear it. Rachel and I

discovered an old town report from Wren that was poorly labeled. That's why we missed it earlier. It was included in an account of a strange rich woman coming to the village and charming the townsfolk—right up until she disappeared with nearly all of the talented people. Among those stolen were a mother and daughter—the mother was a body walker and the daughter a mind reader. It's *us*. My name was on the list. Your full name is Romana Maeve Casares, and it was on there too. There's no doubt."

Maeve sags against the wall, then moves to sit in front of the fire. Her mind races through all sorts of scenarios, too many and too fast for me to keep up, without heed to the careful order she usually keeps.

"That's unusual, for two generations in a row to be talented. And to be so specific to ours…even our names…" Maeve shakes her head, then looks at me again with new eyes. "It must be true."

"That's why I won't run away from you. I know you won't hurt me. I know you won't release my soul, because I'm who you've been searching for."

Tears glisten in Maeve's eyes. Her thoughts reveal how terrified she is of believing me only to find out it's a trick. But with every second that passes, she becomes more convinced.

"It's like we knew. That day when we met. I hadn't intended to take on traveling companions. But there was something about you. Something special." She stares at her hands resting in her lap. "I simply chalked it up to the idea that you must somehow resemble one of my daughters. I never dreamed you actually *were* one of them."

"You had three children, right?"

She looks at me askance. "Yes. But I can't recall their names or faces. Just their ages and that I loved them fiercely. The Lady stole everything else about them from me." Her hands ball into fists.

A choking laugh wells up in my throat. "She let me keep the opposite. All I had left was a list of names. Nothing more."

"She always was a cruel woman," Maeve spits out.

I step toward her, a hint of panic flaring up in my gut, but I shove it down. "I know you're different from her. You found me. You don't need to ruin other people's lives to bring back the others."

She frowns. "But I need them. I need my—our—whole family back. Don't you? We can help each other, Simone. Don't you see?"

Her words cut into me. She isn't wholly wrong. I'd give

almost anything to have my entire family back. To know my father and my brother and sister. I swallow the lump in my throat. But I have no choice but to let them go and try to salvage what little of my family is left instead.

"No, I won't help you hurt my friends in the same way Lady Aisling did. If anything, what you plan to do to them is worse!" I dig my nails into my palms, almost surprised by my sudden outburst. Fury that my own mother would do this floods me.

Maeve looks as though my words have physically struck her. "All I want to do is put our family back together. Why is that wrong?" She points to my friends, now listlessly hovering nearby with blank faces like silent sentinels. "Their minds are weak and terrified. They're barely living the second chance at life they've been granted. If anything, I'm doing them a favor. It's better to use their bodies for people who'll really make the most of them."

Ice begins form into a hard lump in my gut. Somehow she's convinced herself that this is not only the best thing for her, but somehow good for my friends as well. How do you reason with someone who is already so far beyond it?

My hands shake, and I plunge them into my skirt pockets.

"Where did you get this idea, anyway? I don't understand how you would even know this was something that could be done, especially after having been a flower for many years."

Maeve gives me a shrewd look. "You're smart. I'm glad of that," she says. "After I was freed from the garden and discovered my family had vanished, I went to see Lady Aisling. I intended to kill her outright, but she offered to help me instead. I was surprised, but I agreed. We made a deal."

The ice in my belly begins to spread. A deal made with Lady Aisling can't possibly spell anything good. "Why would you do that? You can't trust her. Not for a second. She always has an angle."

Maeve shrugs. "I went in fully aware she was using me, and I know exactly what she's using me for. The truth is I'm using her too. My eyes are wide open. Getting our entire family back is worth any price."

I'm terrified to ask the question I know I must ask. "What was the deal?"

"You don't need to know that. I'm your mother. I'll take care of everything, and you needn't worry about a thing. Come here."

"I'm *already* worried. I need to know what the deal was." I fold my arms across my chest.

She shakes her head. "Fine, I'll tell you. But I have everything under control." She takes a deep breath, and I look into her thoughts almost by instinct. Despite her protests, there's a part of her that's not entirely sure about this deal. I just need to find a way to latch on to that and bring it to the forefront.

But before I can dig deeper, she speaks again. "We agreed to an exchange. She would tell me how to repair my broken family"—she looks wistfully at me for a second—"and I would fetch something for her in return."

"What did she want?" I ask, dread holding me in a vise.

Maeve waves me off. "That doesn't matter. She told me I need to find a soul summoner and that they can be used to bring the dead back to inhabit a new body." Her eyes practically glow with desperate longing. "She told me where they were last seen."

I shudder. "And where was that?"

"As luck would have it, Wren. Your village. Our village, I suppose."

My jaw drops. "Wren?"

"Oh yes. Our missions turned out to be beautifully aligned."

My mind scrambles to wrap around this revelation. The journal she stole from Connor was supposed to be written by a soul summoner. That report Rachel found mentioned a soul summoner who had escaped Lady Aisling's clutches since they were away while she was visiting the village. If that's the soul summoner Maeve seeks, that also explains why she kept that map of where Wren once was located. I just don't understand how that would help when the remains of Wren have long been underwater.

"That's why you were so eager to help us and go to the Archives. You thought we might know something about the soul summoner." My heart sinks into my toes. "You didn't even like me and Sebastian. Not really."

Maeve reaches for me, but I shrink back. "That isn't true. I've grown fond of you both. Wouldn't you like Sebastian to really be your brother? He could be if you help me get him back." Terrible hope lights Maeve's face.

"Never," I say, louder than I intended. She frowns. "Lady Aisling must have wanted something big in return for such information."

Maeve snorts. "You won't let go of that, will you? I have

it under control. I agreed to track down a gift giver for her in exchange."

Horror trickles over me. Gift givers can give someone a talent.

Lady Aisling wants her magic back. And she's using my mother to do it. She's playing off Maeve's desperation and letting her believe she's in control.

I have no doubt Lady Aisling has a plan in place for every contingency. And if she gets her talent back…

I can't even bear to think about the ramifications.

My head aches and I sink down the cave wall, wrapping my arms around my middle. "No, no, no. Maeve, no. That's too awful to even consider. She'll just imprison you and all of us all over again."

"She most certainly will not. I made her shake on the deal and gave her a taste of her own medicine. When she regains her powers, she's promised to leave me and mine alone. And she knows that if she touches my family, I won't hesitate to use her for my own ends."

I shudder. "What if she doesn't keep her promise? What if she gets close before you notice?"

"I won't be taken unaware again, and she knows it."

"But that is so risky."

"As I said, I cannot put a price on the value of my family." Maeve straightens up. "Now, it's late. You should get some sleep. Tomorrow, we'll retrieve Sebastian, and then we'll find the soul summoner together."

She leaves the little cave, stationing Melanthe in the doorway. I try to read my old friend's thoughts, but Maeve is holding the reins too tightly. All I can hear is Melanthe's faint cry for help. She can't hear me. It's unbearable to be this close to my friends and my newfound mother and to know they're all working against me, willingly or not.

I curl up on the floor near the fire, letting tears fall until they're all dried up and I've drifted away to sleep.

# CHAPTER TWENTY-FOUR

The next morning, no light wakes me. Only someone shaking my arm.

"Come, eat. Then we'll go," Maeve says.

I rub my eyes. "Go where?"

"To get Sebastian. Remember?" She laughs. "We're going to fetch him, and then we'll go far away from here now that I have an idea where the soul summoner is."

That makes me sit straight up. "You know where they are?"

"Do you think I would've risked leaving the library if I didn't?"

Of course she wouldn't have. Maeve is always well prepared for everything. It just hadn't occurred to me last night.

"Where are they?" I ask.

Maeve laughs again. "I shall keep that to myself for the time being. But in good time, perhaps I'll share that with you too." She crouches next to me and puts a hand on my shoulder. I force myself not to shudder. "I wish to share so much with you, my precious daughter. But I have to be sure I can trust you first. You're too concerned with things that shouldn't worry you right now, and I'm afraid you might do something rash to ruin my plans."

"What could I possibly do that would ruin everything for you?" All I can do is read minds. While useful, I don't see how that could possibly impact Maeve's plans. Physically, I'm no match for Maeve, if it came down to that.

"It's a risk. And I'm very cautious about risks."

She stokes the fire and begins to toast some bread over it. The smell makes my stomach rumble. My last meal was yesterday late afternoon. When she hands me a piece of toast and some cheese, I tear into it like I haven't eaten in weeks.

Running through the woods and being held captive can really work up an appetite.

We eat quietly, neither of us sure what to say to the other. I can tell from unguarded parts of Maeve's thoughts that she wants to know more about me, but the trouble is that neither of us can remember much about ourselves. Lady Aisling's cruelty only continues to ripple through our lives.

I remain quiet until I can't stand it any longer. Too many questions bubble inside me until I feel as though I will burst.

"Why Euna?"

Maeve frowns. "What do you mean?"

"Why did you take her over? What did you want?"

She laughs and shakes her head. "Access. I took her over several times, but the last was the longest, and the only one she or anyone else noticed."

Now it is my turn to be confused. "Several times? Why didn't we notice?"

"It was just for a brief moment. Long enough to make her say things like 'Let them in' and 'Find them a room.' Or 'Yes, you can have full access to the ancient archives section.'"

My mouth drops open. "She wasn't going to let us in. But you made her say yes. Why didn't she realize it?"

"I took her over just long enough to make it seem as if she'd changed her mind, leaving her surprised and confused but unaware of what really happened. Nearly every time I've done that, the person won't admit it wasn't them. Their minds can't handle that someone else could be controlling them. And they keep quiet to save face to the people around them. Pride is very predictable."

Disappointment fills me. "Oh. I thought Euna liked us, but she only gave us special treatment because you forced her to do it."

Maeve shrugs. "In all fairness, she grew to like you and Sebastian. She just needed a big nudge to let us in the door."

I frown again. "But what were you doing with her that night when we found you controlling her?"

"Again, access," Maeve says. "She can access any room in the Archives—more than any other librarian. In order to get the information I needed, I had to use her."

"Why didn't you just make her change her mind?"

"Because I needed her to take the action, not just say something to make others do something. Even if I made her agree, she'd never actually do it. Taking her over was the only option."

I shudder. It's incomprehensible to me that Maeve can speak of using another person's body against their will in the same manner as she might discuss the best route to the nearest village.

I don't know what else to say, what more I can try to make Maeve see reason. I let my talent wander, seeking out anything living in these caves. Anything that might be useful. I have to warn Sebastian and the others. Maybe even begin thinking about how to escape with Jemma.

At first, all I find are small creatures, mostly insects and bats, and a little warren of wild rabbits and a fox den not far from the cave entrance. I don't know how I could use any of them to help.

But then I find the familiar shape of a human mind. Quite a few minds, in fact. Sebastian and Rachel have returned. And they've brought guards from the local village. My heart soars, but I do my best not to react. I don't wish to give them away.

*Rachel!* I call out to her.

*I'm here*, she responds. *So is Sebastian.*

*I know. I'm with Maeve. She wants Sebastian back. Her plan is to return to the Archives for him. We're leaving very soon.*

I can hear the smile in Rachel's thoughts. *Good. We'll be waiting in the woods to ambush her.*

*Be careful.*

Anxious knots form in my stomach, making it impossible to eat any more. I set the remains of my breakfast down, which doesn't escape Maeve's notice.

"Done already?" She shrugs. "Well, we ought to be going

anyway." She packs up the rest of the food and gets to her feet. "Come," she says, holding out her hand. I take a deep breath and let her pull me up to standing.

I'm not sure how to navigate this strange relationship with my newfound mother, who is also the person I've been fleeing for weeks. But right now, going along with her is the best course. And the safest one for my friends.

To my surprise, we don't exit immediately. Instead she holds me at arm's length and looks at me with a strange expression. One glance at her thoughts tells me that emotion is sincere regret.

"Simone, I know you're not thrilled about me using these other children as hosts for your sister and brother. I'm sorry about it. What you said last night about being as bad as Lady Aisling... I never intended that. I just want our family to be back together again." She rubs my arms in a manner that should be comforting, but all I feel is cold and confused. "If there is another way to get them back that doesn't require me to use your friends, I will do it. I'll see if I can find a way, I promise."

I do my best to smile as if this pleases me. And to be fair, I can sense that she means what she says. But she still doesn't see that what she's doing is wrong, and that's what worries me the most.

She takes my silence as assent and pats my head as she straightens up.

Discovering that I'm her real daughter has only served to make her even more determined to carry out her plan, as I feared. Despite her regrets, if no other options present themselves, she will follow through with her plan. That much is clear.

Maeve reclaims my hand, and I don't resist. I keep my talent on guard, reaching out for Rachel and Sebastian's thoughts. I feel them and a whole contingent of guards a few yards away from the cave entrance. The other shells follow behind us like silent ghosts, still subdued and under Maeve's control. Jemma and Ida, though, are nowhere to be seen. Is Maeve really leaving them behind? Maybe she has other plans for them. With every step, fear tightens around my chest.

How many people can she control at once? Is there even a limit? I hope Rachel and Sebastian are wearing their obsidian amulets. Maeve won't hesitate for a second to take over Sebastian if he isn't. To be honest, a part of me is surprised he's here, knowing how scared he is of the body walker. The rest of me understands.

He's here for the same reason I tried to rescue him last night: I couldn't bear leaving him alone with his greatest fear.

*We're almost there*, I think at Rachel.

*We're ready*, she says.

When we reach the entrance to the cave, morning light streams inside as far as it will dare. We step into the sunshine, and the trees greet us. Maeve squeezes my hand. "See?" she says. "It's a perfect day. Soon we'll be far away from here and won't have to worry about anyone trying to separate us again."

Then the forest erupts.

Guards in silver and green uniforms swarm us, taking Maeve by surprise. One grabs her by the arms, and she simply stares him down. He releases her and attacks the other guards.

"Don't touch her!" I cry. "She uses her talent through touch!" The guards slow their approach as they circle us, cutting off our exit back to the cave. Ropes and netting appear in several hands. Some of them also have obsidian amulets around their necks, but not all. Rachel must have brought every artifact she could find at the library.

Maeve jerks me closer. "You knew?" she says. The hurt in her eyes is unbearable.

"I can't let you do it," I whisper. "It isn't right. In your heart you know this too."

"Let the children go," warns one of the guards.

Maeve laughs. "I don't think so." Suddenly a huge fire-breathing creature lumbers out of the woods behind the guards. Many duck and yell, temporarily breaking the circle that surrounds us.

Natasha's work, but not something they were prepared for.

Maeve yanks me toward the trees while the illusory dragon chases nearby guards, but I wrench my hand free. Her face falls. "You said you wouldn't try to escape."

"I'm not escaping. I'm being rescued," I say.

"But you must come with me. I'm your mother." She lunges for me.

I run as fast as I can. I don't glance back until I'm safely sandwiched between Rachel and Sebastian.

And when I do look back, I wish I hadn't. Maeve's face has transformed into a hard line.

"You tried," Rachel says. "It's all you could do."

*Thanks for coming back for me*, Sebastian thinks.

*Likewise.* I manage a smile that quickly fades as the struggle unfolds.

Maeve still has control of one of the guards, and he prevents the others from capturing her until his fellow soldiers apprehend him. Rocks and branches fly through the air. Melanthe's talent hard at work. Rachel shoves us behind a tree to keep us safe.

Finally, the guards manage to subdue Maeve, catching her up in a net. She struggles and grunts.

"Simone! Tell them I'm your mother. They must let me go. Our family depends upon it!"

Before I can stop him, Sebastian gets to his feet and approaches Maeve with an outstretched arm. She tilts her head at him, as puzzled as the rest of us. But a quick look with my talent reveals all.

"No! Sebastian, don't!" I lurch forward and pull Sebastian away from Maeve. He gives me a confused look.

"Why not? If I remove all memory of meeting us, she'll leave us alone. She'll have no reason to trouble us ever again."

Rachel shrugs helplessly in our direction. "I didn't have time to fill him in on everything," she says.

"First of all, she's looking for shells. Even if you take the memory of meeting us, she'll still keep after us because of what we are. That's how she found us to begin with." I take a deep breath. "Secondly, what Maeve said is true. She is my mother,

Sebastian. She's doing this because she wants our family back. She isn't a bad person, and the fact that she cares about me is the only crack in her resolve to carry out her plan. If you take those memories, we'll have no way to reach her."

Sebastian hesitates. Before he can make up his mind, a terrible sounds rips through the clearing. It's as if the forest has launched itself in defense of Maeve. Thick branches—much larger than the ones Melanthe has thrown thus far—strike the guards. When the sound stops, the four guards who were holding the net are on the ground, dazed or unconscious. Before the rest can even react, a knife dropped in the struggle shoots up into the air, then whistles toward the net holding Maeve captive. The knife makes short work of the ropes, and Maeve slips out unharmed. She gives a hard look at me and Sebastian, then retreats into the dark forest, leaving Melanthe to keep the guards at bay until she's a safe distance away.

# EPILOGUE

**W**e return to the library, safely away from Maeve's influence. The guards managed to capture Kalia and Natasha and bring them with us. Elias and Melanthe were nowhere to be found.

Maeve surely has them.

Still under Maeve's control, Kalia and Natasha resisted at first. But the librarians gave them each an obsidian necklace to ward off any future attempts to reclaim them. Until we can find a permanent solution, they must always wear obsidian or risk being controlled by Maeve again. They're bewildered but grateful. Rachel requested permission from Euna to research ways to permanently break the psychic bond a body walker creates with their victims and was granted it.

Then we can save Elias and Melanthe too.

The librarians have sent for their families, but Kalia and Natasha want to remain here. They want to help stop Maeve.

The guards searched the caves from top to bottom and found Ida and Jemma tied up in a cave deep in the system, farther in than I'd ventured. No wonder the brief hint of their thoughts was so faint. Jemma's horse was found, too, lodged in a stable in the nearby village. According to one of the guards, food and supplies had been going missing every couple of days over the last few weeks. Both Ida and Jemma had been seen in the village acting strangely. As near as we can figure, Maeve was sending them in to the village at night to take things she needed after having them scout the place first. Perhaps her assertion that she had plenty of money was all a lie. Or it was at least ill-gotten.

But now they're free. Sebastian and I are anxiously waiting outside the infirmary for Jemma to get the all clear so we can see her. It feels as if we've been in the hall waiting for hours, though Sebastian keeps telling me it hasn't been that long at all.

To keep myself occupied, I let my talent wander the

Archives, reaching out to brush over the thoughts of the librarians and their servants.

And then—*I'm so grateful they found them and took them in...*

The familiar shape of Jemma's thoughts cuts through the static of all the rest. I give Sebastian a huge grin.

"She's coherent again. That's something."

If thoughts could make people float, Sebastian would be lifted right off his feet.

As soon as we can see her brown curls, Sebastian takes off at a run. I'm right behind him. Seeing Jemma again almost makes it seem possible that everything could return to normal.

In spite of who I am, of who my mother is and what she's willing to do.

Jemma embraces both of us tearfully, and we're ushered into a sitting room and left to catch up. Sebastian begins to tell his sister everything before she's even fully seated in the chair.

"I was worried about you both," she says when he finishes. "I'm glad Maeve found you in the woods and took care of you, but to think that she was the body walker all along... She's the one who...who...took over my body." Jemma shivers.

"What happened after we left you?" I ask.

Jemma's expression darkens. "I only remember bits and pieces. I had just settled with the tavern owner and was walking back to our table. Someone tapped me on the shoulder, and then…I was no longer in control. I fought it at first, but they were too strong. After you two fled, I didn't have the strength to keep fighting. It was like falling into a dreamless sleep."

I shudder. I know that feeling well. But for me it was more like a waking dream. Doing things I didn't wish to do, but without a choice in the matter. Perhaps I experienced it differently because of how Lady Aisling's magic worked with mind-based talents.

"When I was myself again, I was in the woods. I had no idea how I got there, but eventually I found my way out, and not far from the inn either. I was able to collect my horse, but I had to pay extra; apparently I'd lost two whole days. They were ready to sell poor Red off. I started after you, and then… The rest is a blank."

"I'm sorry," I say. Maeve is my mother, and I can't help feeling as if this is somehow my fault.

"You have nothing to be sorry about. You hadn't even met Maeve yet, and had no idea what your real mother was like."

Jemma squeezes my arm warmly. I've missed her. She's kind and warm and honest, all things Maeve is lacking.

"I just… I feel responsible." I shrug helplessly.

"Well, then what do you wish to do, Simone?" Jemma asks.

Determination fills me from head to toe. I've given this a lot of thought over the past few days. I know Maeve is going after the soul summoner, and that there was a soul summoner last seen in Wren before it flooded. She may have gleaned more information than that, but it's a place to start.

"We have to stop Maeve from carrying out her plan. We must save our captive friends and her from herself."

And then and there we promise each other: that's just what we'll do.

# ACKNOWLEDGMENTS

First and foremost, I must thank my readers. Your love and support of the Shadow Weaver series is what made this companion duology set in the same storyworld possible. It quite literally would not exist without you. Thank you so much for reading, and I hope you love Simone's story too!

My editor, Annie Berger, for taking this second journey through the Cometlands with me and Simone and her friends. I'm so glad you love my weird little girls as much as I do! And, as always, none of my books would make it to bookstores without the rest of the incredible team hard at work behind the scenes at Sourcebooks Young Readers, especially Margaret Coffee, Sarah Kasman, Cassie Gutman, Ashlyn Keil, Michael Leali,

Stephanie Levasseur, Lizzie Lewandowski, Heather Moore, Valerie Pierce, Stefani Sloma, Heidi Weiland, and many, many others. I'm so grateful to work with you all.

Super agent Suzie Townsend, for having my back two hundred percent of the time (to some, that may seem like an exaggeration, but if you know Suzie, you know just how accurate it is). And the rest of the team at New Leaf Literary & Media, but particularly Cassandra Baim, Dani Segelbaum, Kathleen Ortiz, Mia Roman, and Pouya Shabazian. I truly have the best team a writer could possibly hope for.

And last but never least, my family. My writing schedule has been completely bonkers, but you've helped me stay grounded and sane. In the end, all these books, all this work, is for you.

# ABOUT THE AUTHOR

MarcyKate Connolly is a *New York Times* bestselling children's book author and nonprofit administrator who lives in New England with her family and a grumble of pugs. She graduated from Hampshire College (a magical place where they don't give you grades) where she wrote an opera sequel to *Hamlet* as the equivalent of senior thesis. It was there that she first fell in love with plotting and has been dreaming up new ways to make life difficult for her characters ever since. She is also the author of the Shadow Weaver duology and *The Star Shepherd*. You can visit her online at marcykate.com.